AFTER LIFE AS WE KNOW IT

AFTER LIFE AS WE KNOW IT

CAROLYN PIERCE

XULON PRESS

Xulon Press
555 Winderley Pl, Suite 225
Maitland, FL 32751
407.339.4217
www.xulonpress.com

© 2024 by Carolyn Pierce

All rights reserved solely by the author. The author guarantees all contents are original and do not infringe upon the legal rights of any other person or work. No part of this book may be reproduced in any form without the permission of the author.

Due to the changing nature of the Internet, if there are any web addresses, links, or URLs included in this manuscript, these may have been altered and may no longer be accessible. The views and opinions shared in this book belong solely to the author and do not necessarily reflect those of the publisher. The publisher therefore disclaims responsibility for the views or opinions expressed within the work.

Paperback ISBN-13: 978-1-66289-541-8
eBook ISBN-13: 978-1-66289-542-5

Table of Contents

INTRODUCTION	ix
CHAPTER ONE	1
CHAPTER TWO	15
CHAPTER THREE	29
CHAPTER FOUR	42
CHAPTER FIVE	63
CHAPTER SIX	73
CHAPTER SEVEN	81
CHAPTER EIGHT	94
CHAPTER NINE	113
CHAPTER 10	126
CHAPTER 11	137
EPILOGUE	145

Introduction

Waking up was always hard for Beth. She had never been a morning person. But now, her only relief came in her dreams. There she could live life as she knew deep in her heart it is meant to be lived. The world of her childhood has long gone, and she now lived in an afterlife that was not welcoming, but hard and deceptively cruel. It was hard not to become bitter in a pessimistic world. How and why did we let it get so bad?

Looking back, Beth couldn't really put her finger on a specific time when she thought her nation was in trouble. It was such a logically benevolent, progressive slide into socialism that it just seemed right. The media led the nation into complacency with their coverage that favored the progressive movement. There wasn't a large protest or any movement to push back on the direction the country was headed. There was a small movement called the Tea Party, but it seemed to run out of steam before it got started. Looking back, one could see how the government, with the help of the media, seemed to lull everyone into a complacent state of mind.

If Beth was to be truly honest with herself, it took the nation a very long time to make the transition from a free capitalist country to a socialist dictatorship. History shows it started before she was even born. Somewhere along the historical road, the United States Constitution was co-opted and turned into something ugly, demeaning, and downright evil. As it was happening, no one was outraged. No one thought it was shocking or terrible. And if they did, they were ridiculed into silence. And no one seemed to care.

Now, the push for communism was in motion, and much like before, no one seemed to care.

CHAPTER ONE

How can such a beautiful morning bring such fear and trepidation? The remaining storm clouds and the rising sun brought a gorgeous start to what was sure to be a long, horrific day. The rain-cooled morning air was sure to be stifling when the sun finally breached the horizon. The heaviness of the air matched Beth's feelings of helplessness and despair. She couldn't breathe, but it wasn't from the moisture-ridden air pressing her down. The phone call from Principal Davis continued to ring in her ears. Ever since all kids were required to go to the publicly funded government schools, Beth had felt like she was losing her children. Now, they really could be lost to her forever.

Adam and Beth did not want their two oldest to go on the citywide band trip to Laredo, Texas, for several reasons, but had no say in the matter. It was too far away from Wichita, Kansas, and neither of them were allowed to go as sponsors. Something in their medical records was flagged by MRD, more affectionately known as Mr. D, a new branch of the IRS. MRD stood for Medical Records Dept. The universal health care plan placed all medical records under the watchful eye of the IRS, which, in turn, had to set up a new department to keep track of everyone's records. Another useless layer of bureaucracy, according to Adam, but they maintained control regardless of public opinion. It was like trying to access the country's most top-secret information to find out what caused their records to be flagged, resulting in their being turned down to travel with the youth. Both Adam and Beth were in great physical shape for their age according to the physician on duty, so their denial to go as sponsors was troubling.

Conner, their oldest son, and their daughter Dawn were excited at first for the opportunity to travel with eighty-eight other band students from area schools. But as the practices progressed and their departure date drew near, they both seemed anxious about the trip. Neither would say why they were feeling the way they were. Beth feared her kids were instructed by school officials not to voice their negative individual opinions about the band trip to their families. Their answers about the trip seemed rehearsed and verbatim to one another.

Just then, Adam stumbled out the patio door with two steaming cups of coffee.

"Good morning, beautiful," said Adam, which was his usual morning greeting to her. "Feels like it's going to be a sticky, miserable day in the neighborhood."

Beth knew Adam was trying to make her feel better about the situation with the kids, but he honestly wasn't helping at all! "Morning," she responded while accepting her cup of coffee. Maybe it would help alleviate some of her worries if she were more awake and could think more rationally about the situation.

"Have you heard anything else from Principal Davis?" Adam asked.

"No. None of the other parents with kids on the trip that we know have heard anything else either. The news on TV only said that the US-Mexican border was officially closed. Davis didn't know if they were stateside or still in Mexico when it happened. He claims he hasn't heard anything from any of our sponsors or the promoters of the trip. The phone lines are jammed and keep going dead. I can't get ahold of any of the numbers we were given in case of an emergency. Even Conner's cell phone doesn't seem to be working!" Beth stopped her rant to hold back her tears. She needed to stay rational for the sake of her kids.

Adam reached over and started rubbing Beth's neck. "I know you're frustrated and scared, Beth. So am I! But we must deal with the now and not the what-ifs. We must stay focused and clear-headed to help our kids when they call. They are good kids. They're smart. They're survivors. They will come home!"

Adam always found the positive angle in every situation. He was the optimistic one. Without the training he received at USMC, he claims he would not have survived the long days he spent deployed to the war zones in the Middle East. That time in his life changed him. He was calm in the face of adversity and danger. He had a peace about him that Beth didn't quite understand, but she was trying to. Beth had to remind herself, if he could make it through that situation, she could manage this. After all, the kids were on the same continent, less than 900 miles away with a group of good students and sponsors. Why haven't they been in touch with anyone at the school? What was our government doing to help them? Why was the border closed? Oh Beth, shut off your brain for a few minutes and drink your coffee! She took a long sip of her coffee and tried to focus on the sunrise that was painting a beautiful morning sky.

She knew Adam was right. However, fear can do paralyzing things to your mind and body. Beth had to keep fighting it, to stay strong for her kids.

According to the itinerary they received when they dropped off the kids, the first day was a travel day. First plane ride for both of her kids, and she couldn't watch their reactions. Another reason to be bitter about the whole situation! Oh well, no use crying over spilled milk, Granny always said. Once they landed in Laredo, the kids got settled into their hotel rooms and made the obligatory phone call home telling their families they were there safe. She thought it was bizarre that Conner didn't have any excitement in his voice. Before he hung up, he reminded Beth to pay attention to her ABC's. What an odd thing to say! She knew he was trying to tell her something but hadn't been able to figure it out. Their family motto was to always pay attention to your ABC's. Kind of silly, but it had to do with their names, Adam, Beth, Conner, Dawn, and their youngest son, Evan. A, B, C, D, E. Paying attention to your ABC's meant you were to pay attention to the family. *What were you trying to tell me, Conner?* She had reminded him to do the same, and his response was: "Always." In a strange way, that gave her some comfort because she knew he was watching out for Dawn.

The next several days were filled with band rehearsals and getting to know the other kids from around the nation that were also participating in this event. They had a few small performances throughout the week leading up to the grand finale. Their big performance was two nights ago at the Laredo Civic Center. The kids were rewarded on the last day of their trip with an adventure across the border to do some sightseeing and souvenir shopping before heading home. The government-controlled school promoted the trip as a unifying exercise to ensure all schools in the nation were receiving the same education in the musical realm.

"Excellence in equality." That was the new unified school motto. If all received the same education, all things being equal, then all could excel. Their logic didn't quite ring true with Beth. She agreed with treating everyone equally, because according to our original Constitution, we were all created equal by our Creator. However, she also knew that people excelled in different areas according to their abilities. For instance, Conner was an avid outdoorsman and very athletic. He was most happy when he was camping or fishing. Dawn was their musical prodigy. She tolerated their family campouts. She was amazing to watch as she found "the music," as she liked to say, in everything.

Conner and his buddy Aaron agreed that this cultural exchange experience was a waste of time. All the girls wanted to do was shop. How boring. It was all souvenirs made in China being sold on the streets in Nuevo Laredo, Mexico. It looked and sounded just like Laredo, Texas. So he had resigned himself to playing a game of tracking his sister, Dawn, and her new friend from Michigan. Aaron agreed that her new friend didn't have the best intentions for Dawn. He was about the same age as Conner and Aaron. Why would a seventeen-year-old want to hang out with a fourteen-year-old? Conner couldn't think of any other reason except to take advantage of her. Conner wished his sister would just hang out with her friend Carly from home, but they were both pretty enamored with Tom, their new friend from Michigan, and had a huge argument over him earlier in the week.

They heard the commotion before they saw everyone running toward them. Aaron pulled Conner to safety in an open doorway just as the masses ran by in full-panic mode.

CHAPTER ONE

"What's going on?" screamed Conner. "Do you see my sister?"

"No, but that jerk from Michigan scampered by looking totally scared to death. He was out of control. He knocked over two girls trying to get away."

"Get away from what?" Conner asked. "Where's Dawn?"

A familiar-looking boy running for his life fell in front of Conner and Aaron. They helped him up before he could get trampled by the next wave of people headed their way. "What's going on?" they asked.

"I'm not sure. Some creepy-looking guys with guns were threatening to open fire on us if we didn't get back to our country! They shot at a group of girls!" The boy was so scared he broke loose from Conner's grasp and started running again.

"Dawn!" Conner started running against the crowd. He had to find his sister! Why had he let her get so far ahead of him? Just as he reached the corner, Carly and Dawn were flying around it at a pace so fast he swore their feet weren't touching the ground!

Dawn was screaming for everyone to run. He grabbed her but, she just fought him off and screamed louder. Aaron caught up with her and knocked her through the entrance they had taken refuge in just moments ago. Conner grabbed Carly as they followed Aaron and Dawn to a brief protection from the seemingly never-ending throng of a terrified mob running for their lives. Just as they fell behind the nearest counter, a gunman ran by shooting randomly, laughing, and shouting for the "Gringos" to run for their lives. A peek around the end of the counter revealed a body of one of the students that had traveled with them from Kansas. What was her name? Her blank stare seemed to be yearning for Conner to remember her so that her parents would know. He couldn't think! Shock and horror were sinking into the dire situation they were in. Dawn started to get up and run again but was stopped dead in her tracks at the gruesome sight in the doorway. She screamed again! Conner pulled her down and covered her mouth so that the gunmen wouldn't hear her and come looking for them. He hugged her tight as she sobbed uncontrollably. "That's Sally!" she moaned.

Slowly, after what seemed like an eternity, it grew quiet on the street with only an occasional gunfire. *What do we do now?* wondered Conner. Should they have kept running with the crowd? How do we make it to the border now? It had to be at least eight to ten blocks away. *Might as well be 100 miles*, he thought. What about everyone else in their group? Were others hurt or killed like Sally? Just then the curtain hanging over a doorway at the back of the store shifted. They weren't alone in the store! Aaron saw it too and started to circle around for a better position to get a jump on whoever was going to come through that doorway.

CHAPTER ONE

The gym was overflowing with a swarm of media outlets, and the families of the students caught up in what was turning into an international incident. Security was tight. Rumors were flying about a high-ranking politician that was going to address the crowd. Adam and Beth had already turned down a dozen requests for an interview. Beth didn't trust the media. They seemed to have an unspoken agenda they were promoting, and it didn't have the country, let alone her children's, best interests at heart. This was to be the first official briefing for them, but they had seen other briefings in the news conferences on TV in other towns where students were from. They all seemed to be smartly choreographed, with no real information provided. Adam thought it was all being downplayed, but he couldn't figure out why. It reminded him of several incidents that he witnessed in Iraq, but to this day would not speak of. All they wanted was their kids home, safe and sound.

Adam and Beth were escorted toward the front adjacent to the stage in an area reserved for family. Principal Davis gave them an awkward glance of recognition but quickly turned his attention to the mayor and the man in the dark suit that seemed to be in charge of setting the stage for the upcoming press conference.

Beth took her seat next to a woman who looked as if she hadn't stopped crying since the news broke.

"How are you holding up?" Beth politely asked. She already knew the answer.

The woman just stared at the floor in front of them, wringing an old handkerchief into knots and then unfolding it, only to do again. Beth hadn't seen an old "hankie," as Granny called them, in a long time. She reached out to put her arm around the woman and silently share in their grief.

She seemed startled at the touch of Beth's arm. "Have you seen my Sally?" she asked.

"No, I haven't. I'm sure she's okay with the other kids in the group." Beth tried to sound as reassuring as she could, fearing she failed miserably.

"I don't think so. One of the kids got a phone call out to his parents when it started. They were running for their lives he said. He saw my Sally fall, then his phone went dead!"

This was very unsettling news to Beth. She hadn't heard of anyone that had had any contact with their children since the incident. "Did the boy say anything about any of the others?"

"He said an older boy helped him up, so he didn't get trampled. He was looking for his sister."

Mayor Browning was starting his opening remarks, but Beth couldn't focus! She sat stunned as the news she had just heard sank in. Was it Conner? Did he find Dawn? Were they okay?

"This is such a trying time for our community and our country. Please be patient as our government officials work out the details for safe passage for our children. I'm sure they will get them home safely," the mayor explained.

Beth wanted to scream!

"So please give a warm welcome to Sidney Jones of the US State Department," Mayor Browning concluded his introduction. Red flag warnings were going off in Adam's head. Why was the State Department involved in a high school band trip? He squelched memories that he wished he didn't have from the war. Things were sounding eerily familiar, except now his family was involved.

"Good morning, everyone. As Mayor Browning said, I'm the court appointed attorney from the US State Department assigned to this case. We are continuing our investigation into this incident, and I assure you, we will get to the bottom of this and get your innocent children home."

Adam's mind was reeling! *What did he just say? Did he just accuse some of our kids of being a part of this illegal smuggling scheme? Shouldn't all the kids be innocent? Who determines their innocence or guilt?*

The attorney continued. "This is what we know as of this morning. The Mexican Police were able to infiltrate a large smuggling operation. This faction would allegedly steal valuable merchandise and then smuggle it with illicit drugs that were hidden in the merchandise into the United States. They would target unsuspecting American tourists to carry the merchandise across the border. It is apparent that some of the children from your schools here in the

Wichita area were used in this scheme." Loud objections erupted in the gymnasium at the possible accusations being leveled at their children. Adam was furious! *Their kids were targeted and used to smuggle drugs unbeknownst to them. And they were the possible guilty ones in this?*

Jones continued to speak louder to be heard above the murmurings. "That is why we agreed to fully cooperate with the Mexican government and close our border. This was done to keep the perpetrators in Mexico so they could be brought to justice in the country where they have allegedly committed their crimes. Mexico has in custody all the students and the sponsors on this excursion except for four students from the Wichita area. Everyone is cooperating fully with the Mexican authorities, and we believe they will soon be released to American officials. They will be transported to an undisclosed facility in the United States where they will be given the opportunity to call home. They will be afforded comfortable housing and food. Unfortunately, as per our agreement with Mexico, they will not be allowed visitors or the opportunity to come home until all the perpetrators have been arrested and brought to justice. This is for their safety. These gangsters will stop at nothing to make sure all witnesses to their crimes are silenced, permanently." Sidney hated his job right now. This crowd was angry and soon would go ballistic over the next news that he had to share.

"Your children were innocent spectators who happened to be in the wrong place at the wrong time. Unfortunately, one child was caught in the crossfire. Her body will be sent home after an autopsy is performed to determine the exact cause of death." For a brief second, you could have heard a pin drop. Then an outburst from angry, scared parents filled the room. Everyone in the press scampered to get the first question asked and answered.

Mayor Browning and several security personnel stepped to the edge of the stage as if to calm the crowd. Sidney Jones continued, "We will release the student's name once her family has been notified. Listen, people, I know you're scared and you're very worried about your kids. We are doing everything in our power to get them home safely to you. Once all your children are in the protection of our government and the smuggling ring and drug lords involved are incarcerated, you will get your children home safe and sound."

This was the most news released to date by the government about the unfolding situation their kids were caught up in. It still didn't ring true to Adam. Why now were both governments cooperating and cracking down on smuggling rings and drug lords? The black market of stolen goods and drugs had kept the American economy from going over the cliff into a total collapse for several years now.

The border with Mexico had been like a sieve with illegal immigrants crossing daily. *Why was the border closed now? Is this our new reality?* Adam bellowed his question so loud that it momentarily silenced the crowd.

It was the question they all wanted answered. "When will we get our kids home?"

Chapter Two

It would be dark soon. Dawn hated the nights. All she wanted to do was go home. How long had it been since she'd seen her mom? Their trip was only to be one week. The day before they were to head home was a nightmare that wouldn't stop playing in her mind when she tried to sleep. That was four days ago. It seemed like an eternity.

According to Conner, they were still in Mexico, but she wasn't sure anymore. They were constantly on the move. Sleep deprivation was playing cruel tricks to her mind. Conner seemed to trust the family that rescued them the day her world fell apart. At least they were feeding them, even if it wasn't very much. So far, they had kept them hidden from the authorities, who seemed to be working hand-in-hand with the drug cartels.

"Sir… Sir… Mr. President…"

"It better be good, Tony; I haven't slept in over thirty-six hours!" snarled President Zimmerman.

"Yes, sir. I'm sorry to bother you, but President Santos is calling again."

Frank Zimmerman was just starting the second term of his presidency, and he hadn't had a good long night's sleep since the election. He had to remind himself constantly why he ran for office! No one in their right mind would want this position. Not in its current state at least. Hopefully, that would all change soon, and he would have full control of his destiny, not "the people."

It really hadn't been up to him ever since his college days at Harvard. His career seemed to be choreographed from forces out of his control. A process to fundamentally change the world, to enforce the interests of a ruling class at all levels, socially and economically, was in play. Frank was smart enough to realize he wanted to be in the ruling class and not the working class. He joined a group called the Brotherhood of Social Justice. From the very beginning, they were a perfect fit for Frank. He wanted to make a difference in the world, leave it a better place for his children than what it was when he was young. In his mind, too much capitalism was polluting the world, destroying Mother Earth. The rich were getting richer, and the poor were getting poorer. It had to stop! If the world could learn to all get along and work together for the common good, all could achieve their inner happiness and the natural resources could be saved and replenished to sustain humankind forever.

CHAPTER TWO

He was also taught that the United States, being the leading capitalistic country, the world's sole superpower, was the largest roadblock to achieving world peace and prosperity for all. The Brotherhood had tried for years to destroy the economic machine of the United States from the outside. Finally, they learned it would have to be fundamentally changed from the inside to achieve real change. Frank Zimmerman knew he was the man to make those internal changes happen. He was well on his way to achieving the goals set out by the Brotherhood: he would save the world from the evil capitalism that had been promoted by the old United States. His name would prevail in history, songs would be written to honor his glorious triumph as the man who prevented the world from the total devastation that was sure to come if the masses still had the freedom to choose their destiny.

People just couldn't admit their stupidity and their need for a savior. Frank remembered his parents taking him to church as a child and their belief that a Savior indeed was needed, and that Savior was Jesus, a man who lived a couple thousand years ago and was crucified for His teachings. He proclaimed He was the Son of God and came to save the world from their sins. All one had to do was believe in Him, ask Him to forgive them for their sins, and then commit to follow and serve Him the rest of their days. How foolish were his parents and all that believed the Bible and this man's teachings! The Brotherhood had shown Zimmerman that the world does need saving, but only humankind can save the world, not some mythical god that surely did not exist. He was honored that they chose him to be that leader for such a time as this!

Rugged individualism had to be squashed if the entire population of the world was to achieve greatness. No one could achieve more than another. A ruling class would have to be formed to guide the masses into group euphoria, enjoyed by all equally. Of course, the ruling class would have to be compensated accordingly for bringing world peace! Frank deserved a piece of that pie. He would help influence change that would truly alter the face of the world.

Having the president of the United States working for their cause was truly an ingenious plan launched by the Brotherhood for Social Justice years before Frank became a Harvard student. Frank's charismatic personality and his speaking abilities led him into a role of a prominent mouthpiece for the Brotherhood. Unbeknownst to Frank, early in his college career, they started grooming him for the presidency. Not because his ideas were any good but because he was easily manipulated to do as they wanted.

Frank picked up the phone. "This better be good, Eduardo!" snapped President Zimmerman. "Tell me you've resolved our problem with the four missing kids from the Excellence in Equality band trip."

"We're getting close to a resolution, Frank."

"Call me President Zimmerman!" Frank yelled. "I think I've earned that title!"

CHAPTER TWO

"Call me President Santos then! I know I've earned it!" Eduardo replied angrily. His mind raced. *Why do all Americans think they're so much better than the rest of us? I know Zimmerman's true objective, and he treats me like a child! He's so out of touch, he doesn't even know he's being played!*

With a heavy sigh, Frank apologized, sarcastically. *At least he's beginning to realize I can't be manipulated like the flunkies in his administration*, thought Eduardo.

Frank knew better. He knew he needed to treat the president of Mexico as if he belonged on the big stage of life if he was to get him to manage the problem they were facing with the missing kids. But Eduardo was just exasperating!

"You said you're close to a resolution. What is it?"

"My intelligence agency tells me they're still in Mexico. In fact, they're still very close to Nuevo Laredo, where they went missing. We can apprehend them within the next twenty-four hours. That is if I can get five million American dollars per child to the drug cartel leader."

"What?" screamed the president. "I can't authorize that. We don't negotiate with terrorists!"

"They're not terrorists." Eduardo replied calmly. "They are my intelligence agency, like your FBI or CIA, only they work to improve our import and export opportunities that grow our nation's economy. Just think of it as an opportunity to improve *our* relationship. We would be more open to advancing the secret coup of your government you have in the works with the Brotherhood of Social Justice. We can call it a down payment for the compensation of past wrongdoings by your country to mine over the last three hundred years, give or take a couple years, of course."

Frank was stunned! How did Eduardo know about their plan to bring the United States into the new order of the global community? "Let me think about this."

"You have until tomorrow morning. Otherwise, the children will be caught in a deadly drug deal that will go horribly wrong, if you know what I mean. I'm sure that would not be good news for you or your cause. Something like this could cause civil disobedience. Something like an uprising of the conservative whackos that you so want to bring into the lemmings group."

"By the way, Frank, how is the reeducation camp with all the other kids going?"

Frank was boiling mad now. How did Eduardo know about that? Although that was the whole reason for the band trip in the first place, no one outside of the Brotherhood knew about it. All the kids were to be detained at the border and taken to a special camp for their "safety" until the drug cartels that did this could be apprehended and brought to justice. The kids chosen for the trip weren't randomly selected as per the information given to the parents. These kids, if swayed to follow the plan, should be persuasive enough to get others back home to follow. If they couldn't be converted to the cause, they would "contract" the deadly strain of the disease

CHAPTER TWO

commonly known as TB breaking out in Mexico, a new strain that is supposedly drug resistant. They would then be quarantined until their eventual deaths. That was the whole reason for this trip. Was Eduardo a member of the Brotherhood? Frank had a hard time believing that. If he wasn't, the only explanation was a massive leak of information, a whistleblower that would need to be found and eliminated, quickly!

"Mr. President, you have until six o'clock tomorrow morning. Otherwise, I can't guarantee the kids' safety." With that, Eduardo hung up on the president of the United States. *Man, that felt good,* he thought!

Frank ordered a pot of strong black coffee before getting into the shower. He wanted to be more awake and alert for the next call he had to make.

"Wake up, Dawn," Conner nudged his sister.

"We must go, now! Juan tells me we can cross the border tonight. He's going to go with us because he's done it before," he explained to Dawn and Carly.

"But I'm so tired," whined Dawn. "Why can't we get a good night's rest and go tomorrow night? We've been here so long, surely one more day won't matter."

Aaron was getting annoyed with Dawn's complaining. She really was a baby! "You've been whining about wanting to go home and couldn't understand why we weren't going anywhere. Now we have the opportunity to go, and you're still moaning about everything! Grow up, Dawn! Remember, they're looking for us, and they probably want to kill us!"

"Well, how do you know Juan won't lead us into a trap? Why do you trust him?" Dawn argued.

"Come on, guys." Conner was tired of always being the peacekeeper. He knew if they were to survive their journey home, they would have to figure out a way to get along. The last four days had been crazy. By some miracle, Juan found them hiding when the chaos broke out. Conner was positive Juan saved their lives. He felt a connection with him that he couldn't explain. They seemed to know each other's thoughts. Their perspective of the situation was essentially identical. Something was terribly wrong in the world, and they were small fish caught up in a larger plot that neither could quite figure out, but both instinctively knew was erroneous, with an evil undertone that they couldn't put their finger on.

Conner sensed this for some time now. He thought his dad sensed something wasn't right either. Whenever he tried to talk to him about it, he couldn't get him to open up. It was as if he was trying to protect Conner, still seeing him as a little boy. But he wasn't a little boy anymore! After all, he was sixteen, almost seventeen, but felt like he was going on thirty. How was he going to keep their group together so they could survive what was sure to be a horrible trip?

CHAPTER TWO

According to Juan, his government was working backdoor deals with the United States for the illegal immigrants to go across the border unimpeded to sway elections. Conner thought the elections had been fixed for a long time, and now it seemed he was right. The illegal drug business was booming on both sides of the border. Both economies were teetering on the edge of another great depression, so both governments turned a blind eye to the drug cartels. Juan also knew of a larger plot that was well underway to secretly overthrow the US government. His older brother got involved with one of the drug cartels and overheard stories of the coup that would overthrow the US government and combine their two countries into one. He told his family but soon after was caught in the crossfire of one of the many cartel battles. Juan suspected he was murdered for what he revealed to his family but couldn't prove it or convince his father to believe it. Although his father wasn't convinced of the pending coup, he did see that something was terribly wrong. He helped Juan plan the border crossing to get the four Americans out of Mexico. If his oldest son was right, he had to get Juan out of Mexico also. Conner had to get home and tell his dad about all they suspected. As a former Marine, he would know what to do and who to contact in the government to help stop it and save their countries.

Conner had had enough of his sister's attitude too. "Why did you trust that nitwit from Michigan? He left you behind when the shooting started. Aaron and I are the ones who came looking for you and Carly. We're the ones who have protected you through all this. We're the ones to continue protecting you so we can all get home. But you have got to stop questioning every decision I make. You must trust me, Dawn. Remember your ABC's."

Dawn knew her brother was right, but she was terrified. All she had ever wanted to do was play music. Now all she wanted was to be at home with Mom and Dad. Not go on a survival expedition. This journey wasn't going to be easy, and she knew it. Conner was good at camping and hunting. She wasn't. In fact, she hated it. He was working on his Eagle badge for survival preparation in the Boy Scouts before they closed the organization due to discrimination charges that she didn't quite understand. She knew he would do everything to get them home, but fear can paralyze and mess with one's judgment.

With a big sigh she said, "Okay, Conner."

Another sigh. And then, "I know Mom and Dad would expect us to stick together, but just remember I'm so stinking scared I can't seem to think straight!"

"I know, Sis. I'm scared too," admitted Conner. "But I know we can't stay in Mexico, so the only option is to trust Juan to get us safely across the border and find our way home. We can't trust anyone. Except ourselves."

"What about Juan?" Carly asked.

"He's one of us now. He's going with us, all the way." Conner didn't want to share why Juan had to talk with their dad; not yet anyway. It would send his sister and Carly over the deep end!

Juan led them as quickly as possible through the side streets of the sleeping town, always staying in the shadows, trying to stay quiet. The shadows seemed to have a life of their own; it was their safe zone. And yet, the shadows were the creepiest place to enter. What else was hiding in the darkness? Their eyes would play tricks on them. What was that moving? Was it really moving? It was a slow process. Conner knew they only had to go about seven blocks, but it felt like seven miles! Stopping. Hiding. Running. Crawling. Waiting. Staying as quiet as possible—all easier said than done! Especially for the girls. One minute they were trying not to laugh, and the next they were fighting back tears. There seemed to be drug cartel members out in force, looking for trouble. Or were they looking for them? Dark, sinister characters. One could usually smell them before you saw them. All were armed for a major battle.

Once they reached the Rio Grande, you could see America on the other side. The kids felt as if they were almost home because surely there would be help for them on the other side of the river. Conner, however, was suspicious because of what Juan had told him. None of them knew the dangers that lay ahead. Sometimes being naive can be a blessing. Sometimes it's almost a curse. They found floating debris that had somehow been staged by Juan for their use to hide themselves as they swam across the river. Also hidden in the debris was fresh drinking water and food for a day or two if rationed properly. They split the supplies equally between the three guys. The girls only had a bottle of water to worry about. The river water was dark and cold. It had a nasty smell of rotting fish, or at least that's what they hoped it was! They had to go slow without making too much of a splash. The smell would almost gag Dawn and Carly at times, especially when the water splattered on their faces. It would get on their lips and get sucked into their mouths. If they were spotted on the river, they would be easy targets. The current was strong. They used it as much as possible to make it look as if the debris was just floating along and not being propelled across the river. Conner and Aaron worked hard to stay close to the girls without too much commotion. Juan seemed to be able to cross without any trouble. It was obvious he had done this many times, just like he said he had.

Conner noticed the ICE agents on the American side were not looking the other way as Juan said they would. This was obviously a new procedure for them. They looked menacing in their starched uniforms with weapons at the ready. Were they looking for them too? He was sure of it. Once they reached the American side, he had hoped they could find safety with them! But Juan was nervous and told him again that they couldn't trust anyone, especially the border patrols.

"Remember, we can only trust ourselves," Juan whispered.

CHAPTER TWO

Once Frank Zimmerman hung up the phone, he breathed a huge sigh of relief. That wasn't as bad as he assumed it was going to be. The Brotherhood had certainly done their homework and planned for every possible scenario in this situation. He would call President Santos about thirty minutes after his deadline of 6:00 a.m. He was going to enjoy reminding him that the United States doesn't negotiate with terrorists. Better yet, he would insinuate that Santos himself was acting like a terrorist. Hopefully Santos will have acted on his warning and unleashed the drug cartel on those kids. The threat of cutting off the billions of dollars in foreign aid to Mexico should help keep Santos in line. Frank was confident he had everything under control.

Technically, the Brotherhood had everything under control, but Santos didn't need to know that. Wasn't Frank a part of the Brotherhood? So he could say he was in control and not be lying. The fate of those pesky kids was not important. Whether they're killed or not by the drug cartel, the US would put out the story that they had been rescued successfully and would soon be reunited with the rest of their group. ICE agents were notified to apprehend the kids on sight. Rumors within the agency of the possible exposure to a deadly disease would ensure their capture to be clandestine and swift. After all, they wouldn't want to jeopardize citizens. And if the agents became suspicious, they would be exposed also and silenced with the rest of them.

It would be to their benefit if those kids were killed in Mexico. Not as messy. There would be a lower chance of their bodies ever being recovered to reveal the truth. The reeducation had not gone well at all, so plan B had been implemented. If the kids did not go along and lead the way for all the kids back in their hometowns to accept the fact that a new USA was coming, then they were no longer useful and would have to be eliminated. All the kids selected to go on the "Band Trip" were now deemed as the true troublemakers in their respective schools. They weren't assimilating to the new truths being taught about the United States and the absolute necessity to bring about the new global order. The four missing kids weren't present at the camp for the controlled exposure like the rest of the group. Frank didn't understand why plan B hadn't been the original plan. He told them it would have to be utilized. Grieving parents will be so much easier to manipulate.

President Zimmerman's agenda would include coordinating with the CDC and his health agencies on how to contain the "mutated strain of tuberculosis" that was occurring at the camp where the rest of the band trip participants were being held. Timing of the release of this story would be critical. The four missing kids needed to be neutralized immediately.

Chapter Three

Beth awoke to the sound of knocking on the front door. Sharon, Sally's mom, had finally fallen asleep after the horrible news of the death of her daughter. She hoped Sharon hadn't heard the knock. She needed to sleep. They were becoming fast friends. *Why do we have to wait until our world is crumbling to get to know our neighbors?* Sharon lived just two blocks from Beth and Adam. She had moved to Wichita soon after her husband was killed in the Middle East wars. Her family didn't want anything to do with her since she married a "warmonger," and his family blamed her for their son's death. She had no one except her Sally. And now, she really had no one.

When Beth looked out the window to see who could be knocking at such a late hour, she saw only a package by the door. She immediately called Adam. After his stories from the war, she knew better than to open the door.

After their long, cold swim-float across the Rio Grande, the kids were exhausted. The smell of the river lingered in their clothes making everyone feel sick to their stomachs. Juan wouldn't let them rest though. He wanted to put some distance between them and the river and the border patrol agents. Juan also knew they were close to a train and truck depot. If they could get there and into a freight car without being detected, they might just have a nice, long ride inland.

"Is everyone okay?" he asked.

"Other than being exhausted and smelling like dead fish, I think we're good," responded Conner. Dawn and Carly looked totally worn out. Hopefully they wouldn't start whining. Aaron was putting on a good face, but Conner could tell he wasn't feeling very well either.

It looked as if they might have an hour or two before the sun came up. Conner knew they had to get undercover quickly if they were to avoid being spotted. The brush seemed thick by the river, but he instinctively knew that was not a good place to seek shelter.

"Now what?" Conner asked Juan.

"We have to get out of sight fast," responded Juan. "There's a train depot close by. If we can get there, we can rest and possibly get a ride north away from the border patrol agents."

After some grumbling from the girls, everyone agreed to get to cover before they stopped for the night. Juan took the lead with Conner bringing up the rear. He made sure

CHAPTER THREE

none of their clothes got snagged on the underbrush and their tracks were erased as much as possible. He didn't want to leave a trail. Zigzagging through the thicket was necessary but slowed their pace. He was afraid they would run out of time and lose the cover of darkness. One could hear the trains up ahead, coupling, and uncoupling cars, with whistles blowing occasionally.

The thicket was getting thinner, allowing them to pick up their pace but also exposing them more to the border patrol. Juan stopped at the edge of a clearing. Once they were all crouched together, Conner could see the nearest train car was at least a full football field away.

"How do we cross this without being seen?" Aaron asked.

"We must be quick but quiet. I think if we go in two groups, we'll have a better chance of not being seen. Plus, if we are seen, we have a better chance of all of us not getting caught if we split up. Aaron and I will go first and find a car that's open. Then we'll signal for you guys to come," said Juan.

"Okay. Make it quick. I don't want to get caught out here when the sun comes up," quipped Conner.

The boys took out at a fast run crouching a bit as they went. They made it! Soon they were out of sight between the freight cars. Carly and Dawn were getting nervous. "What if they don't come back for us?" Carly asked.

"They'll come back. Aaron is my best friend. He wouldn't leave us."

Dawn asked the next question. "What if Juan knocks him out and abandons us?"

Fatigue was causing Conner to doubt his new friend's intentions. "He wouldn't do that!" was his response to the girls, but secretly he wondered about it himself. Things seemed to go like clockwork with Juan. What if he was leading them into a trap? No! He had important information about what was happening, and he seemed to be genuinely concerned about the direction his country was taking. Same as Conner's fears about the United States.

Stay calm, Conner, he told himself. *Get to safety now, rest, and then figure out the next step.* "Carly, I want you to make a run for the cars, aim for where the guys went. When you get there, wait for me and Dawn. Can you do that?"

"Absolutely!" And she was off, just like that. Her speed surprised both Conner and Dawn.

"As soon as she gets there, Dawn, we're going to make our run, okay?" He did a quick scan of the surroundings and didn't see anything suspicious.

"Okay, but I can't run very fast. Not like Carly."

"Me either, Dawn. We'll go at the same time, and we'll stay together. We'll make it!"

Carly made it faster than the boys did. "Let's go, Dawn!" They took off as fast as they could but soon tired. They were about halfway across when Conner heard a car motor. Was it heading in their direction? He couldn't see anything, no headlights headed their way, but there was definitely a motorized vehicle driving in their vicinity. Was his mind playing tricks on him? Dawn tripped and fell, scraping her knee. She let out a small, anguished cry as he stopped to help her up.

Once she was up, they took off again. Trying to quicken their pace was a necessity but very painful for Dawn. Conner was impressed that his sister seemed to be running faster than before. They saw Aaron and Juan join Carly. The last twenty yards seemed to be the longest, but they made it just as the car lights came into view.

"Hide!" Juan led the way and climbed under the nearest car and then seemed to disappear as he crawled up into the undercarriage of the train.

Within a matter of seconds, they were all hidden. The vehicle seemed to slow down as it approached. It stopped! They could hear both car doors open and two sets of footsteps milling around where they had just crossed.

"I can't believe we finally have orders to shoot border jumpers on sight! Wish we could have been doing this all along," said one of the border agents.

"You misunderstood the orders, Pete! Again! We're only to shoot those four American kids with our taser guns if they won't stop when told to. They've been exposed to some bad virus bug thing. We can't let them expose all of us! We're not to approach them unless we're in full hazmat gear. You did pick up your hazmat suit, didn't you?"

"Well, how do we know the Mexican jumpers haven't been exposed too? I say we shoot them all and ask questions later! I can always say I thought it was one of those bratty American kids. They should have stayed with their group! Then they'd all be in quarantine."

One of the agents stopped right where Conner was hiding. He held his breath hoping he wasn't going to look under the car. Just then he heard the man's zipper and saw the steady stream of pee as he relieved himself, washing away the blood drippings from Dawn's scraped knee from when she fell.

"I heard there's no cure for this virus bug they're carrying. Sounds like most, if not all, the kids at the camp aren't expected to make it. Half of them are already dead, Pete! That's bad! Real bad! You may be onto something about shooting first and asking questions later."

The agents headed back to their vehicle when they heard their radio dispatch calling them for a check point. Just as quickly as they appeared, they were gone. The sun was breaking the horizon ensuring another scorcher of a day. The kids slowly dropped from their hiding places, all stunned at the conversation they had heard. What virus bug thing? Quarantined? Their friends sick, dying or dead?

"What were they talking about, Juan?"

"I don't know. There's been rumors of a mutated strain of TB going around that is supposedly drug resistant. But I thought it was manageable, or fake news. We must get into that freight car up ahead and hope we can get far away from the border today!"

CHAPTER THREE

"Isn't it going to be hot in the car?" moaned Dawn. "Hotter than outside of the car?"

"Possibly. But they were coupling it to other cars, so it looks like it's going to be moved. Once we're moving, the breeze will help cut the heat. We must get away from the border agents and away from this disease."

"What about my knee? It's really starting to throb, and I'm leaving a blood trail."

Conner was impressed his sister picked up on her blood trail. He tore his shirt sleeve off and quickly wrapped her knee. "Let's get undercover, and then we'll take a good look at it."

Aaron led the way to the freight car that was going to be their mode of transportation. They quickly scrambled up inside and were barely settled in when they started to move, slowly at first. Soon they were moving quickly through the town of Laredo heading toward home. After washing Dawn's knee, rewrapping it, and a quick breakfast of protein bars, the girls nestled together and in no time were fast asleep. Aaron and Juan soon followed them to slumber land. Conner wanted to stay awake to process all the information they had overheard, but the motion of the train was making him sleepy. Maybe a fresh mind would be better to think more clearly, he reasoned as he drifted off.

Adam slowly approached the front porch, seeing the package by the door. This made him anxious, as it reminded him of IEDs left by the roadside in Iraq. He knew the wheelbarrow that he was using for a shield wouldn't do much for him if the package was a bomb, but it made Beth feel better knowing he had something to use as protection from a blast. As he got closer, he noticed the official stamp from the MRD, the government's new branch of the health agency that handled everyone's medical records. Why would Mr. D send packages to them? Why didn't the person who brought it wait for them to deliver it?

He was close enough to see that the package looked legitimate from the outside. A note attached to the front was visible, so Adam pulled it off. It was an explanation as to what the package contained and why they just dropped it off. It had to do with the virus that they were talking about in the news. The theory was that the kids were exposed to it in Mexico, but the CDC was using an abundance of caution just in case the families were exposed in the States. The government didn't want to expose more people unintentionally and risk spreading the disease further. It was safe to assume if Sharon had received a package from Mr. D, they probably had one sitting on their front porch too.

As Adam picked up the package, Beth opened the door. "Is it safe?"

CHAPTER THREE

"I think so. It's from Mr. D. I think it has information about this disease they're saying the kids have been exposed to." Adam brought the package inside for Sharon to open when she woke up. The neighbors were beginning to gossip openly because of the stories in the news about the kids and the band trip. He could feel their eyes watching him with the package. The looks they were getting were changing from concern to fear and possibly anger that their families somehow jeopardized the neighborhood.

Granny may be right. It may be safer for them to go out to her place, away from the city. Beth didn't want to leave though, because of Conner and Dawn. She reasoned if they came home, she wanted to be there for them.

Conner woke when the train came to a complete stop. Where were they? He looked out through the slits in the siding and saw they were at another train depot. He could tell by the sun's placement it was still early in the morning. This means they hadn't gone very far. Where were they? He woke up Juan to ask him.

"Oh man, we're at the main train depot in Laredo on the west side of town. It's larger and will have border agents with dogs. See the rail over there? It comes across the border from Mexico, so they patrol this one a lot. I didn't realize we'd have to come through here."

"What do we do?" wondered Conner.

"Let's stay put for now. We're out of sight, so we're safe for the time being. Let the others sleep. You and I can take turns on watch. From the looks of the other cars we're hooked to, we should be headed north soon. I can take the first watch if you want."

Conner was exhausted, and he knew he needed sleep. "Okay, but wake me at the first sign of any trouble."

Adam and Beth were almost home. The walk from Sharon's was making them both feel better. "Exercise and fresh air have a way of doing that for you," Granny always said. Sharon had slept for a couple hours but got up soon after they brought the package in. She took a quick shower and came out to the wonderful aroma of freshly brewed coffee. After a few sips, she insisted Adam take Beth home so she could get some rest too. It was going to be another long day filled with fear as the events of the last several days penetrated further into her consciousness. She needed to start planning for Sally's funeral when they finally released her body to her. At least she had the comfort knowing that Sally didn't suffer. A bullet in the head tends to bring death instantaneously, unlike the other kids now being held in quarantine because of this rare, mutated, drug-resistant disease. Sharon never thought she'd be thankful that Beth's kids were missing.

CHAPTER THREE

But that possibly meant they might have a chance to avoid this awful illness.

Sharon turned her attention to the package. The note said it had information about the illness and medicine to take in case they were infected but not symptomatic yet. It also said there were several N-95 masks to be worn in public until further notice and a testing kit to be administered as soon as possible. As she opened the box, her finger came across a razor-sharp point making her pull her hand back quickly. A small red trickle confirmed she had cut herself. What was that smell?

Beth answered her phone on the second ring just as they entered their yard, seeing the package on their porch.

"Beth, don't open your package!" screamed Sharon. The fear in her voice stopped Beth dead in her tracks.

"What's wrong, Sharon?"

"The package is leaking awful smelling fumes. I cut myself when I opened it too. Beth, I don't feel so well."

"Adam, we have to go back to Sharon's!"

"No! Stay away! I think…I don't…know…I…" Beth heard the thud of Sharon falling out of her chair. What she didn't know was that Sharon was dead before she hit the floor.

Adam had heard the last part of the call too. Although he was stunned, his military training kicked into high gear. Beth was going into shock and crumbled to the ground. Adam knew instinctively they were being watched. He helped Beth up as he quickly scanned the neighborhood.

He kept hearing a soft buzzing. How long had he been hearing it? It was just now registering with his brain that something wasn't right about the sound. As he lifted Beth, he saw it. It looked like a small bird fluttering around their sycamore tree by the street. He'd seen these in Iraq. Why was a small drone tracking them? A better question was, who was watching them?

Events were happening quickly now. President Zimmerman knew he had to keep the situation under control if they were to stay on schedule. There had been many strategy sessions about how this part of the plan would go. The lemmings were sufficiently subdued by the passage of drug legalization laws coupled with the lack of employment throughout the nation. There was no reason for them to clear their heads from the drug-induced stupors. The video games and television shows were great reprogramming tools for the people. Most were unaware of the manipulation being perpetrated on them. The best part was that they didn't care.

His problem was with the old-school patriotic nut-jobs who still believed their lives should be full of freedoms to choose how they wanted to live. Those were the ones that still believed there was a God who cared for them more than the government did. They were the idiots who believed hard work and capitalism was the way to prosperity. They didn't care about the little guy. All they wanted was to make money for themselves, take care of themselves. The goal was to systematically take them out without raising suspicion. The band trip fiasco was becoming a great start to the elimination of these weirdos. Grieving parents would fall in line nicely, he assumed. Frank would not allow their stupid patriotic duty to get in the way of his greatness.

President Zimmerman would be addressing the nation tonight on all media outlets. It would be carried throughout Mexico as well since the crisis involved both countries. President Santos was falling into submission quite nicely. He saw the big picture and knew if he wanted a piece of the action, he would have to do as he was told. Zimmerman could control him. The rest of the world would be tuning in as well. This step was the last transition to usher in the new global society under the leadership of the Brotherhood for Social Justice. He was the face of the new-world order. His chest puffed with pride as he relished in the thought of his role in the world today and how he could really effect the change he wanted. The world needed him. The Brotherhood for Social Justice needed him. But in reality, no one cared. Zimmerman really wasn't wanted or needed.

Chapter Four

"Clickity clack, look at Jack. Clickity clack, don't look back!" chanted Dawn as Carly snickered.

"Clickity clack, look at that. Clickity clack, don't look back!" Dawn was hitting her sing song stride now. "Clickity clack, go to the rack. Clickity clack, don't look back!"

For a brief moment, Conner thought he was back at home and Dawn was being her usual annoying self, not letting him sleep. But why was he hearing a clickity clack? What new instrument was she using now? Why was the room rocking back and forth? "Shut up, Dawn!"

"Clickity clack, Conner's back. Clickity clack, don't look back!" They all laughed this time as Conner opened his eyes to see them all staring at him.

"Where are we?" As soon as he asked reality flooded back, and he knew. They were moving again. *That's good*, he thought. He lifted himself up to look out through the slats of the freight car. The countryside was flying by. How long had he slept?

"Morning, sleeping beauty! Or should I say afternoon?" Dawn poked him in the belly, just like she did at home to irritate him. "We're rolling now! Rollin' rollin' rollin' clickity clack, don't look back!"

"Juan, fill me in on what's happening since my sister can't seem to form an intelligible sentence."

As Conner sat up, Juan handed him a piece of jerky and a bottle of water. Whoever left the food supplies knew what to pack for quick energy on a hard journey. "I don't know how much I can tell you. I'm ashamed to say I fell asleep too. I woke up about an hour ago to your sister's annoying song. I can tell you we're on a track that's running parallel to I-35 that goes all the way to San Antonio."

"That interstate goes all the way to Wichita! We could ride this all the way home if it keeps following the interstate!" said Aaron. "I woke up for a bit while we were still parked. You were both snoozing pretty good. There were border agents everywhere, searching all the cars looking for something or someone! I thought we were busted for sure. But when they were still a couple cars away from us, there was a big commotion on the other side of the yard. It sounded like a bomb went off! Naturally, they all took off running. Then, probably five to ten minutes later, we started to move. I tried to stay awake, but between the motion of the train and being so tired, I don't think I made it out of Laredo before I was asleep again."

"Clickity clack, don't look back! We're going home, Jack!" Dawn sang her new song over and over again. She always found the music.

"I don't want to be pessimistic because right now, this train ride is a very good thing. But I don't think we'll be able to ride it all the way home. They're specifically looking for us, remember? They think we've been exposed to this new disease, and if we're spotted, they will quarantine us immediately. None of us are sick or acting sick, so I think it's a bogus story. Just in case though, we all must promise if any of us start feeling bad, we must let the rest know. Deal?"

Nothing like my brother to cast a huge black cloud over our situation, thought Dawn. *Why can't he just enjoy the moment like the rest of us?*

"Come on, guys! We've got to stick together and be open and honest with each other if we're going to make it home. If they're putting this story out in the media, not only will the cops be looking for us, but so will everyone else. We can't trust anybody! We need more information about what's happening. I'm not sure why, but they don't want us to make it home. Does anyone have any ideas about how we could get a message home or find out more information about what's going on?"

Aaron was the first to speak up. "You're right, Conner. We stick together, no matter what. When we make it to San Antonio, we can look for a coffee house with free Wi-Fi. We can get what the media is saying and search the back rooms on the net for the true story of what's happening. Maybe even get a message home."

Carly spoke up next. "I'm in. I think we ought to try to change our appearance somehow."

CHAPTER FOUR

"Oh, I like that!" exclaimed Dawn. "I've always wanted to dye my hair, but Mom wouldn't let me!"

"What do you say, Juan? Are you in too?" Aaron asked.

"I just want to be sure that you all know that this is going to be a very hard trip. Everyone is looking for us. Everyone will fear us. Something bigger is going on here, bigger than we know. I can't quite figure it out, but I think the powers that be think we're a huge threat to their plan, so they will do anything to stop us, to silence us."

"What are you talking about, Juan?" Dawn feared his answer but knew the question had to be asked.

Juan looked at Conner wanting assurance to proceed or an exit strategy to stop the conversation. He got an assuring head nod, giving him permission to proceed.

The president was livid! How could those kids have made it across the border? Where were they now? Somebody would pay for their inadequate job performance! If Frank had his way, it'd be Mexico's ridiculous president. Frank was sure the Brotherhood would agree with him that Eduardo had messed up one too many times.

The open border arrangement with Mexico was going to have to change. It had served its purpose of slowing down the US economy almost to the tipping point. The Brotherhood of Social Justice had enough new "voters" that would ensure their candidate's election if they had to have another election before the coup is completed. The plan was to suspend elections for a couple of years to establish the new government. The story of the bogus mutated TB virus coupled with the drug cartel smuggling operation being exposed should be enough to activate martial law, which would be sufficient to suspend elections. Frank was guaranteed by the Brotherhood that he would be the last president of the old US of A and the first president of the new USA, the United Socialized Americas, encompassing North, Central, and South America as we know it.

The bigger problem was the terrorists from the Middle East coming across the border with their caliphate propaganda. There was an attack on the main train depot in Laredo that GIM was taking credit for. GIM stood for the Global Islamic Movement, the latest and greatest terrorist group. It really wasn't a new group. They just liked to keep changing their name so that the dumbed-down masses wouldn't realize it was the same group, same ideology, and same goals—total worldwide domination. Their religious beliefs taught them that Allah wanted them to rule the world. Didn't they understand that the plan of the Brotherhood would take care of them too? A utopian society with communism as the sole government worldwide would solve so many of the world's problems. He was forming an idea to allow these fanatics a faux position in the new administration to pacify their ambitions. That really was what they wanted. Frank didn't care because he knew there was no God or Allah or whatever they wanted to call it.

His immediate dilemma was to find those kids from Kansas and silence them for good. The last intelligence report said they were traveling with a kid from Mexico. His immediate family had been found and already eliminated. How many of the extended family remained was unknown. He had suspicions that a lot of them fled already. At least they were scattered, unable to plot and work to undermine the plan for a worldwide government. The official story was that the family had been killed in cold blood by the drug cartels. He had to sufficiently scare the others into submission so that Mexico would come willingly into the new United Socialized Americas. If the Mexicans thought that the drug cartels were out of control and that the United States could provide peace and security, the formation of a unified government could be achieved quickly and efficiently. The people didn't need to know that the drug cartels were working for the United States government as of three days ago when they negotiated a better deal than that fool Santos was offering them. *Our ancestors were so stupid to give it back to them after the Mexican wars*, he thought. Once the countries were united, there won't be a border issue. One more huge ugly problem that my legacy will show I solved, President Zimmerman believed. The rest of Central America would follow Mexico's lead. South America should fall quickly also. Their economies were in such a depression that they would do anything the Brotherhood told them just to survive.

Life is good, Frank thought. *I love it when a plan comes together*! He grinned at his own wittiness and grew prouder of what he was accomplishing and how history would show him to be the greatest world leader ever to live.

Juan wasn't sure where or how to start his explanation of what he thought was happening. He first reminded them of how great their country, America, used to be. It had been the light of the world. Everyone wanted to come there because of their freedoms, their God-given freedoms. Their inalienable rights. He explained how such freedoms afforded people the opportunities to achieve their personal dreams. The American Dream was what drew people from all over the world to their amazing country. Their founding forefathers were brilliant! They set up a government with restrictions on their leadership, not the people.

Time, arrogance, and greed had eroded the founding forefathers' true vision of a government that was to be governed by the people, for the people. Men who probably started out with good intentions let the power of a big government corrupt their thinking, and thus their actions had taken a very long time to erode the freedoms given to the American people in their Constitution. The free republic of the United States of America had been changed from the inside to a socialist society. The socialist movement sold itself as a society whose focus would be exclusively on the well-being of the people. At its core, it drew attention to the social problems caused by capitalism and strived to negate these issues by making everything fair for everybody. Fairness meant no one would be allowed to exceed anybody else's achievements. Instead of focusing on everyone striving to achieve their best, which in turn drove others to achieve higher goals, it concentrated on making sure all were at the same level. This caused no one to try their best. Excellence in equality.

"That's our school's motto!" Aaron pointed out.

"That's right," Conner agreed. He was glad Juan was taking his time to give a history lesson as to why they were where they were. That would make the rest easier to understand.

"My papa had discovered a plot being implemented by our governments to work together using the drug cartels as their fall guy. The goal is to drive our countries to unite under a banner of communism."

"What? No way?" Dawn objected to this idea.

"It's true, Dawn," Conner said, confirming Juan's statement. "Socialism is always just a stepping stone to the final goal of communism. But I also think it's bigger than just Mexico and the US. When you look at Europe, Asia, and Russia, even the Middle East, they all seem to be merging into centralized regions. For communism to work, everyone must be a participant. If you're trying to sell a utopian society that has everyone equal and everyone has a share in everything, then everyone must be in, regardless of what it costs. No personal property rights, no right to defend yourself, no freedom to speak your mind, and no freedom to your religion. It all must be the same for everyone. With countries merged into regional areas, it'd be easier for the leaders to control the masses."

Juan could see the light bulbs turning on in their minds. They were beginning to see the truth in what they were hearing. He could also see the fear beginning to set in.

"So why are they after us? Why was our group attacked in Mexico?" Carly asked the question they were all beginning to wonder about.

"Because I believe they think that grieving families are easier to manipulate and control than ones who still have hope in their children."

"Wow, that's harsh, Juan!" Aaron said.

"Think about it, guys. Our dad is head of security for all the plane manufacturers in Wichita. He oversees the logistics and security needs of all the plants. Plus, he's a former Marine. He received a Purple Heart and Congressional Medal of Honor for something that he refuses to talk about. He's a trained warrior. He knows how to fight. He knows how to train people to fight. He knows how to lead people into battle. And most importantly, he knows how to win those battles. I know he senses some of this too because I've seen it in his face. Juan must talk to Dad. But if two of his kids are gone, they're banking on the expectation that his desire to fight will be broken. He won't fight. He'll do everything to protect our younger brother Evan by being submissive to their rule." Conner was on a roll now. "Aaron, your dad is the president and CEO of the largest bank in the Midwest. They need to control the finances at every level if this plan of theirs is going to work. Carly, I just realized I don't know what your parents do."

"My dad works with the electric company in Wichita, and Mom is a nurse."

"Of course! They need to have control of the utilities for their plan to work. If you're good workers, you have power, life is good. If you're not, life can be rough."

The train was beginning to slow down. "I think we need to get off the train before it gets into the heart of San Antonio. They'll be looking for us. I like Carly's idea to change our looks a bit. We also need to get information about just how serious this disease thing is and if we need to be concerned about getting sick."

Dawn spoke up, "I want to talk to Mom."

"I agree, Dawn. We must let our parents know we're okay. But we must be careful. They're probably watching our parents."

Looking out of the freight car they could see they were probably going to be stopping soon. Juan opened the door to look out. A small town was on the horizon. There was a field of tall corn coming up. It would be perfect to hide in if the train slowed enough for them to jump without getting hurt. "How's your knee, Dawn?" Conner had almost forgotten she had been hurt.

"Oh, it's fine. I've scraped my knees worse when I was a kid learning to ride my bike!"

"That's my girl! We're tough just like our dad. Oorah!"

"Oorah!" Dawn and the rest echoed Conner's bellow of the Marine's call for action.

The field was upon them, and the train had slowed significantly. Juan jumped first and rolled as he hit. He hoped the others did the same. They couldn't afford anyone getting seriously hurt. Carly jumped next doing a barrel roll and came up running toward Juan hiding in the field. The boys and Dawn made their exits with no incidents either. They took off at a fast pace into the field.

They could hear a car before they saw it. A road must be up ahead as they neared the far edge of the field. Conner went ahead while the others rested a bit. There wasn't much traffic on the road, which he liked. The road sign said Devine, TX. Two miles. He could see Interstate 35 to the right of them. Another corn field was on the other side of the road that would give them cover as they got closer to the town. He signaled for the others to join him, and they quickly crossed the road to the safety of the next field.

They made it to the edge of the town quickly. It was your typical small country town. Everything shut down at sundown. The high school was on the edge of town, which Aaron thought would be a good place to try and spend the night. Plus, they would have Internet access, so they could possibly learn more about what was happening with their friends in the quarantined camp and their families back home. Carly said they would likely have some food in their kitchen too, which would be good since they were all starving. They waited about an hour for the sun to start setting to make their way to the school building. All the doors seemed to be locked, but one classroom on the backside had a window that had been left open. Dawn was small enough to squeeze through it. She quickly let the others in.

They crouched together at the end of the hall and listened. The school was eerily quiet. *Guess that's a good thing*, Conner thought.

"Okay, girls, you're in charge of finding food. Don't turn on any lights. We need something to eat now, and we need food and water that we can take with us. Look for some backpacks or book bags that we can use to carry it in. Juan, go with the girls, but I also want you to scope out the school. Look for anything you think will be useful and that we can easily carry with us. Knives, rope, flashlights, matches, tarp or blankets, maps or a compass, cell phones or radios, anything. Aaron and I are going to find their computer lab. We'll get online and see what's really going on."

"Does anyone know what day it is?" asked Carly.

"It's Friday, I think. Why?" responded Juan.

"Well, I sure wouldn't want to be here in the morning if it's a school day!"

"Good point, Carly!" Conner loved how they were all starting to think strategically. The little things could become a huge deal for them. "Let's meet back here in thirty minutes. Everyone look for a school calendar so we'll know if anything is happening tomorrow here."

They headed down the hall and discovered that the third classroom on the left was the computer lab. Aaron and Conner entered as the others kept going. The junction at the end of the hall showed another long hallway leading to what looked like more classrooms. The left hallway opened into a huge common area with what looked like the main entrance to the school and the administrative offices. Juan thought there might be a nurse's office that would have some good items for them to grab. Past the common area was another hallway that had doors further apart leading them to think it was possibly the cafeteria and/or gym. They passed the offices and opened the first set of double doors. It was the cafeteria, and the kitchen was on the far end.

"Girls, go on ahead to the kitchen. I'm going to see if I can find anything in the office area. I'll catch up with you in ten minutes."

With their backs to the windows, Aaron, and Conner both turned on a computer. Conner would research news stories to see if he could figure out what the public was being told. His main goal was to find out anything about them, the disease, the others in their group, and most important, their families. Aaron, who was savvier on the web, would look for the real story in the back rooms on the web. How were the events of the day really unfolding? The faint blue illumination from the screens sent a dull glow out the windows not detected by the boys.

Carly was stuffing an ice cream bar in her mouth. "Oh man, Dawn, this is so good!"

"I know! Mine is delicious too!"

As they ate, they accumulated food supplies on the counter. Bottles of water and juice, fruits, nuts, protein bars, and small individual boxes of cereal were piling up. "There are chicken nuggets in the freezer. Do you think your brother would mind if we cooked them in the microwave? It would be so good to have something hot to eat tonight."

"I agree! Let's do it!"

They heated up more than enough for all of them and started looking for a way to carry their food supplies. Again, the dull glow from the microwave exposed that someone was in the school.

Juan was having trouble with the offices being locked. He had found the nurse's station and was trying to pick the lock. He wasn't very good at it. The administrative assistant's desk revealed a set of keys for all the offices in the bottom drawer. Juan was able to unlock any door he wanted. Inside the nurse's station by the door, he found a first aid kit filled with Band-Aids, splints, Tylenol and ibuprofen, ice packs, burn treatment ointments, disinfectants, and instructions for CPR and other small injuries. *Definitely taking this,* he thought. As he continued searching the offices, he also found two flashlights, a set of walkie-talkie radios with extra batteries, some kid's confiscated cell phone, cigarette lighters, and the school newspaper with the school calendar printed on the back page. Before he left, he grabbed a couple of blankets from the nurse's station and a backpack for all his goodies. He was careful to relock everything to not make it very evident that anyone had been in the offices. As he was putting the keys back, he noticed a fat envelope shoved to the back of the drawer. It was filled with cash! Bonus! He smiled at himself for his good fortune. Hopefully everyone else was having the same luck that he was.

As he left the offices, he saw the girls with their food packs. They were trying each locker as they passed them. Most were locked, but a few were open. They had been able to collect about $30.00 in cash, another cell phone, and an iPad.

"Good thinking, girls!" He smelled the chicken nuggets and realized he was starving. He started eating his share as they continued searching the lockers.

Entering the computer lab was a happy reunion. They all excitedly shared their goodies and explained how each treasure could be beneficial. The chicken nuggets didn't last long, and the ice cream bars were gone in an instant. Their moods had relaxed to the point that if you didn't know what was going on, you would think this group was just a regular bunch of kids hanging out at school, having a good time.

With full bellies, Conner and Aaron started sharing the news they had been able to find. Conner shared first. "Well, the good news is the tensions between Mexico and the US seem to be easing a bit. The disease that they say everyone was exposed to is an advanced strain of tuberculosis that is drug resistant to current treatments of TB and much more deadly. It kills within one to two weeks from exposure. They're working on a new vaccine and cure. Also, they're not sure they have it contained at the detention center where they took the rest of our group."

"Wow, I don't remember anyone being sick around us, do you guys?" Carly asked. "Juan, do you know anything about this strain of TB?"

"I'd heard rumors about it, but my family and I never saw anyone that we thought was sick or might have it."

Conner continued, "The bad news is all but thirteen people from our group at the detention center have died from it."

This news stunned them all into silence for a few moments. Dawn was the first to speak. "Our friends, all but gone? What are the chances of those thirteen who are left? How do we know we're not infected and that we're going to die too?" She started to cry. Carly was already crying. Even the boys were fighting tears.

"Think about it, guys. No one was sick. Then mass chaos as we were chased from the streets. After they're all taken to a safe place, they all get sick? Something's not right with that story."

"You're right, Conner." Aaron spoke up. "I've found several stories suggesting some kind of conspiracy. If the kids aren't conforming to the teachings of the new federalized school curriculum, they are being eliminated. In Alabama, for example, the schools in the Huntsville area had over 800 kids die because they ate school lunches that were tainted with salmonella. What the story didn't talk about was the surge in civil disobedience among the kids because of the rewriting of American history."

"Oh man! Do you think this food is safe to eat? After all, it did come out of their cafeteria?" Carly asked the question they were all thinking.

"Don't panic, guys." Aaron was trying to calm their fears. "I haven't found any such stories linking to any Texas schools. But we must be careful. For some reason all kids, including us, are being targeted."

"Okay, so that's what's going on with this illness story. And as I said, the border issues seem to be calming down. The next story that I found interesting was about the explosion Aaron heard at the Laredo train depot. It seems there's a new terrorist group calling themselves GIM. That's the new Global Islamic Movement. It's not a new group. Same bad guys, different name. They apparently blew up some refrigerated freight cars. The cars were

CHAPTER FOUR

filled with food. Mostly beef and pork products. I think they tapped into the Alabama story and they're trying to create a food shortage. That could generate mass chaos and anarchy as people fight for what little food is left."

"Any news from home?"

"There were some stories about the parents grieving for their children. I must admit, I was surprised there wasn't much more about them. And what's even stranger; we are now dead according to the headlines that will break in the morning!"

"Wow, I guess out of sight, out of mind," Dawn quipped. We must get ahold of our parents. They will go crazy!" With a puzzled look Dawn then asked, "What do you mean tomorrow's headlines will report we're dead?" She glanced out the window to make sure no one was there.

"Why would they put the story out that we're dead?" Carly wondered out loud.

"They control the media. They control the story and the timing of it." Conner speculated.

"Well, if we're dead, we can't talk. We can't tell them that this TB outbreak is phony. We can't tell them that the drug cartel is working for the government. We can't warn people about the silent coup that's in the works to move us into a government that rules via communism. We can't expose their lies if we're dead." Juan explained. "If the story is that we're dead, then they will kill us on sight, no questions asked."

"I agree. Any ideas, Aaron, as to how we can get in touch without drawing too much attention to ourselves? Or putting our families in danger?"

"Well, there are some chat rooms that are creepy, but there are some that although on the surface seem absurd, they might be a safe area to send coded messages. The question is, Will our parents see it? And if they do, will they understand it?

"Let's try. Put up a post that says, 'Paying attention to your ABC's is always a good thing.' If Mom and Dad see it, they'll know it's us. They'll at least know we're still alive." Conner looked at Dawn and winked, giving her a reassuring smile.

"What about a message to my parents?" asked Carly. "Add to it, 'ABC's are electrifying!' And for Aaron, say, 'Bank withdrawals are moving quickly.'"

"I like it!" Dawn said. That is cryptic enough to sound stupid, but our parents should see the connection. Juan, what about your family?"

"End the message with, 'Hasta la vista, baby'; they'll know it's me."

Charlie was enjoying his nightly routine on his front porch. The katydids were singing already with a few crickets joining in. As the sun went down, the lightning bugs started showing themselves. He loved this time of day.

CHAPTER FOUR

It always transported him back to a simpler time. A time when America was free and strong, the absolute best place to live this side of heaven, as his daddy always said. He was thankful his dad didn't live to see how far the country had fallen. He feared for his grandkids. What kind of future did they have living under an oppressive communistic government that was sure to come if it wasn't stopped?

Charlie had lived a full life, he felt he had nothing to lose, so he would do anything to help restore a country that would give his grandkids a chance to experience and achieve their own American Dream. Being delegated as the school janitor was supposed to be a punishment from the local authorities. In their minds, he had been too vocal from his pulpit about the issues confronting their nation. His freedom of speech had crossed over to the dark side, according to the papers. That article always made him chuckle because it made him think of the movie *Star Wars*. The writer must have been a huge fan of Luke Skywalker! The town was following the country's lead by enforcing the freedom of religion clause of the Bill of Rights and shut down his church. Charlie tried to explain how the Constitution states that citizens had the freedom of religion, not the freedom from it. Although he was shunned in town, he had to contribute to the good of the community if he wanted to be included in the allocation of food and utilities. He was still allowed to live in his home that he had paid off twenty years ago, according to his mortgage papers. However, he technically didn't own it anymore. It belonged to the community. It always amazed him that for the rejection he faced around town in public, a lot of town's people secretly told him they were glad he was the school janitor. They asked him to keep an eye on their kids. They always asked him to pray for them, their kids, their town, and especially the country.

He saw his lowly position as the janitor as a godsend. It gave him an opportunity to talk with the kids. *If this country was to be saved, it would start with the kids*, he thought. He was sure that was why kids were targeted so heavily with propaganda in the classroom.

"Martha! I think someone is in the school!" Charlie could see the back of the school from his front porch. He wasn't sure at first whether he saw a light in one of the classrooms. But then he noticed something in the kitchen. It soon went out. As it got darker, the glow from the classroom got brighter. As Martha came out to look, it went out.

"I don't see anything, Charlie."

Chapter Five

Adam didn't want to bring their package from Mr. D into the house, but he knew he had to do something with it. They were being watched; he was sure of it. He also didn't want some kid, especially Evan, their youngest son, to accidently get ahold of it. He would be waking up soon, so he had to do something quickly with it. Beth had finally calmed down enough and was dozing on the couch. She was adamant; she didn't want the package in their house. Holding his breath, he picked up the package and brought it inside. He had placed their trash can by the door, so he put the package directly into it. Quickly closing the door with his foot, he then ran to the bathroom and exhaled deeply and inhaled again. Finding a dust mask from his workshop, he put it on and went back to the trash can with its deadly refuse. He pulled the drawstrings on the trash bag, tied them tightly and lifted it out of the can. After double-bagging it, he found a hiding place in the garage to store it until he could figure out what to do with it. The next step was to scrub his hands like a surgeon. Following a thorough scrub of the hands he stripped down and threw his clothes into a paper bag. He would burn it later today. Then he jumped in the shower. Twenty minutes later, he finally felt clean.

Beth began to stir on the couch. Pouring a cup of coffee for her, Adam went to her and gently started stroking her hair. He needed her to get it together before Evan came downstairs. Beth opened her eyes and smiled at Adam. He was so good to her. She didn't deserve him but was so thankful for their love. Realization of the morning horrors started to push their way into her mind. Adam saw the fear returning to her eyes. He leaned forward and gently kissed her and whispered for her to remain calm; he had taken care of it for now. They had to stay strong for Evan. He didn't need to know about this new dilemma.

"Go take a shower. There's a paper bag in the bathroom. Put your clothes in it, and we'll burn it later today. I'll go get you something to wear. I want you in the shower before Evan comes down. You need to get it together because he doesn't need to know about this."

"Okay. What did you do with the package?"

"It's hidden in a safe place. Now, get your lazy bum into the shower!"

He pulled her up gently, kissed her again on the forehead, and then gave her a tender shove toward the bathroom.

She came back for her coffee and playfully swatted him in the arm. Why couldn't things be like this all the time? No worries. Nothing crazy going on in the world.

CHAPTER FIVE

Beth was thankful for her husband. He was her rock in this crazy upside-down world they were living in.

Adam started to fix a quick breakfast when Evan stumbled into the kitchen.

"Morning, son."

"Morning. Where's Mom?"

"She's in the shower. Want to eat a quick bowl of cereal with your dad before you go to school?"

"Nah, I think I'll just have a Pop-Tart. Have you heard anything about Conner or Dawn?"

"No. But no news is good news, right?"

"I guess." Evan grabbed the Pop-Tart as it came out of the toaster.

"Is this your last day before your summer break?" Adam knew this was the last day of school, but he was trying to make conversation so that Evan wouldn't dwell on the awful situation they found themselves in. Adam thought Evan was acting weird. Or maybe, he was the one acting weird. After all, he had just hidden a deadly package.

"Yeah, it is. Doesn't seem right without Conner and Dawn here. Who's going to take me fishing for the next couple of weeks? Who am I going to pick on if Dawn doesn't come home soon?" Evan was fighting back tears. He didn't want to cry again in front of his dad.

Adam went over and gave Evan a huge bear hug. "They'll be home soon, son."

"What if they're sick? No one knows where they are, so who's going to take care of them?"

With the mysterious packages received, Adam was beginning to think the kids weren't sick. At least not yet. But he couldn't tell Evan about that—not yet.

"They'll be home soon, Evan. They're strong and healthy. And they're smart. I have no doubt we'll all be together again soon. What would you think about heading out to Granny's next week when school is recessed for your two-week summer break?"

The kids loved going to his mom's little farm. It was close enough to get to in a couple of hours and yet far enough away that you really felt that you had escaped from the hustle and bustle of the city. She was still allowed to live on the 300 acres that had been in the family for generations. It had some great hunting spots and a little stream, great for fishing. When she passed, the government would determine the next tenant. She was still allowed to collect income from 260 acres leased out to the neighbor farmer who raised wheat. It helped provide a small income to her meager government check. It used to be called Social Security, but when it became obvious that the bankrupt system was beyond saving, President Zimmerman changed the name to Collective Assistance and cut the payments in half to the people receiving their checks. Once they passed away, there would be no more payments, to anyone. A bill had passed last year in Washington that land would pass into the collective database at the passing of the owner. No one was allowed to own land anymore. It wasn't fair to the ones that didn't have it. Everything had to be fair and equal if they were to achieve peace and security. At least, that was their theory. This would enable everyone to coexist in harmony as a new global society. Everyone had to contribute to the system to get a paycheck. There was no more retirement that Americans had grown accustomed to. You were allowed to leave your job that you had worked at in your prime earning years, but you had to transition to a position that would still allow you to contribute to the community. Most of the elderly now filled the menial positions such as school janitors, lunch aids, bus drivers, door greeters at department stores, or fast-food workers. If you couldn't work, you had better have family that could take you in and afford to have you. However, this move often triggered a detailed examination of the family's assets leading to confiscation of their assets to the collective property fund for future distribution to achieve fairness in equity. Otherwise, death came quickly through the withholding of foods and life-saving medications. Starvation was a slow and cruel way to die. Illness always preceded death. Rumors went that when elderly people were taken to the hospital for whatever reason, they were given "life-saving" treatments that usually resulted in their untimely death within forty-eight hours. No one past the age of seventy went to the hospital unless they had a death wish. Unfortunately, many had that desire, for they tired of living a life that was the opposite of their childhood, and not wanting to be a burden to their families drove people to make terrible decisions.

"I'd like that, Dad, but what if Conner and Dawn come home and we're not here?"

"Well, your mom was wondering that too. I'm sure we'll be notified when they're coming home so we can be back in time to welcome them home."

"There are rumors at school that they may quarantine our neighborhood. They think some of us might already be exposed to this deadly virus going around."

That was news to Adam. "When did they tell you that?"

"Oh man, Dad, you can't repeat that!" Evan looked scared. "We weren't supposed to say anything. They don't want panic in the streets."

Adam couldn't believe they put that much pressure on the kids, telling them not to say anything that might potentially kill their families. "Evan, if we're to survive, as a family, we can have no secrets. We must communicate. We must pay attention to our ABC's. Understand?"

"I know, Dad. It's just so hard because they keep telling us things at school that don't make sense, but we can't talk about any of it."

This truly was disturbing to Adam. Were they trying to brainwash the kids? It sure sounded like it.

"I tell you what, Evan. Why don't I call Principal Davis and tell him you don't feel good and you're going to stay home today. It's the last day before summer break anyway. You won't do anything but clean out your desks and tell everyone to have a good summer. Would you like that?"

CHAPTER FIVE

"I'd love that, Dad, but you can't. They'll come quarantine our house, and then Conner and Dawn won't ever be able to come home!" Evan was fighting back tears again.

Adam reached over and gave Evan another big ole bear hug. He was getting angry again about the pressure they were putting on the kids. It wasn't right. It wasn't necessary either!

"Okay, son. I want you to go to school. Put on your 'everything's great' face. Do as you're told and come home straight away after school. I'll talk to Mom. Maybe we'll head out to Granny's today after school. Our secret. Okay?"

"Sounds good, Dad."

"See ya, Mom." He hollered as he passed the bathroom, grabbed his book bag, and went out the door.

It was all over every news station; the four missing American kids had been gunned down in cold blood by some gang members who had ties to the Mexican drug cartels. Aaron's dad, Tom, knew he shouldn't be surfing the back rooms of the web, but if he was going to find out what really happened to his son, he figured this was the best place to look. There was one chat site that he felt was strange but not totally wacked out. As he was scrolling through the online message board, he was stopped dead in his tracks. Could it be? How could it not be? For the first time in a week since this nightmare started, he had a glimmer of hope that the kids were okay, for now.

He quickly printed the message and then logged off. He had to go see Adam and Beth.

Beth peeked out the window before she answered the door. She knew Tom was hurting as much as they were. Not only was he their banker, but he was also their friend. Now they had a stronger bond in the fact that their boys were missing.

"Hi, Tom," Beth greeted him as she let him in.

"Is Adam here?" he asked.

"Yes, I'll get him." She wondered if he had gotten a package too.

Adam came down and greeted Tom with a handshake. "How are you holding up?"

"As well as can be expected, I guess. How about you guys?"

Tom just shrugged. "Okay, I guess. Did you hear the news this morning?" Beth didn't like the sound of how this conversation was starting and thought she better sit down before she fell again.

As Tom was breaking the horrible news reports about their kids, he handed Adam a piece of paper. Adam could tell Tom didn't want to discuss the note, so Adam allowed Tom's recount of the news coverage to play out while he read the note.

"Adam, what do you think about doing a fundraiser to help raise money to bring our kids home for a proper burial?" His statements didn't match what he was reading. His jaw dropped in shock. It looked like a garbled message. "Paying attention to your ABC's because they're electrifying. Bank withdrawals are moving quickly. Hasta la Vista Baby!"

"What do you mean, Tom? I don't know. Shouldn't the government or school help with that?" His puzzled look implored Tom for more information. He saw Beth's face turn ashen as the tears started to flow.

"Well, maybe you're right. I just need to do something to help. I'm probably grasping at straws. Looking for answers in all the wrong places, I guess. I need to keep busy, or I'll go crazy! I need to develop your patience and trust in our authorities." As he spoke, he jotted down the website where he found the message and handed it to him.

"I know, Tom. We keep looking for ways to help too. We'll come up with something. I need to believe that, or I'll go crazy!"

They shook hands again, and Tom gave Beth a hug as he left.

Adam was ecstatic! He motioned Beth to not ask anything but handed her the note. He was sure Tom had just found a message from their kids. They were alive! And they were coming home!

Tom must not have gotten a package like they did. Otherwise, he would have signaled him about it. He knew Tom was lonely since his wife died last year from cancer. His sons were all he had left. His oldest was away at college, OSU, he thought, down in Oklahoma. If the kids were traveling, they would probably try to reach Aaron's brother first.

The news put a bounce in Tom's step. He would have to mask his excitement today. Beth was doing a small jig. She figured out the hidden message too! Adam grabbed and hugged her tight. He reminded her that no one could know about this. After all, the news media was telling about the gruesome murders of their kids!

"I told Evan we could go see Granny this weekend. I think some fresh air away from the city would do us all good. What do you say?"

"I agree, Adam. It will help Evan tremendously. Plus, Granny will love seeing all of us. She's been so worried about Conner and Dawn. Family time out of the media's eye is just what we need." Suddenly, Beth's looked changed to horror. "Oh, Adam, we must go get Evan. He can't hear about the kids' deaths from somebody at the school!"

"You're right! I'll go get him now. He's been so good through all of this."

"He is good," Beth said.

Adam responded, "All the time."

Chapter Six

Conner woke up first. Something didn't seem right. He felt like someone was watching them. As he sat up to look around, he saw Charlie sitting in a chair by the door with a shotgun draped across his lap. How in the heck did he get a gun? Is he part of the local Sheriff's Department? The old man looked as if he was asleep. Everyone was still sleeping. He figured if he could quietly get up, he might be able to get a jump on him before anyone else stirred.

As Conner started to move, Juan opened his eyes and saw the old man.

"Morning, boys," Charlie said to them.

His deep voice woke everyone up. Carly let out a small scream. Conner assessed the situation, trying to decide whether they could get the better of this one old man without getting shot.

"Don't be scared. I'm not going to hurt you, and I'm not going to turn you in. If I'm not mistaken, you guys are all over the news. You all look pretty good for being dead!"

Charlie slowly stood and stretched as the five kids just stared at him in disbelief. So the story they saw last night was true. Aaron was kind of hoping it was all a big mistake or some sick joke.

"I'm Charlie by the way. Your local school janitor. Saw some lights in here, probably from the glow of the computers last night and figured I better come check it out before someone else did." Conner kicked himself for being so stupid. After he made sure no one used the lights, their computer usage busted them.

"Come on. Martha will have breakfast ready in ten minutes or so." He started to leave, but the kids just stared at him.

"Look, kids, I'm one of the good guys. You're in a heap of trouble. They put the story out that you're dead, so now every law enforcement agency and every criminal will be willing to shoot first and ask questions later. If you want to live, come with me. NOW!" His booming voice commanded their obedience, and yet the kindness in his eyes reassured them it was safe to follow him.

They followed him across the open field behind the school to a small house with a white picket fence surrounding the yard. Usually, yards consisted of nice green grass, but this one featured a big garden with wonderful-looking fruits and vegetables. Back during World War II, this would have been called a victory garden. There was cantaloupe, strawberries, watermelon, cucumbers, tomatoes, onions, green beans, corn, peas, okra, and several types of squash. Next to the fence stood a couple of apple and pear trees. Around the corner and out of sight were peach trees and some sandhill plum bushes. The backyard consisted of a chicken coop and a small lean to shed that sheltered an old milk cow and some pigs.

"Wow, I think we stumbled onto Old McDonald's Farm," joked Aaron. Everyone was snickering until they saw Charlie's wife, Martha standing on the front porch.

She let out a resounding belly laugh and greeted them by saying, "EIEIO, welcome to the farm! Come on in, breakfast is almost ready."

As they entered the house, it seemed smaller than it looked from the outside. But after a quick sweep of the room, one could see why. There were canned vegetables everywhere. There were also two small freezers: one in the front living room and one in the adjoining dining room. The house smelled wonderful! It reminded Conner of Granny's house. Bacon was sizzling along with eggs and pancakes. The aroma of coffee also permeated the air. Again, the kids were reminded of just how hungry they were.

"The bathroom is off to the right of the kitchen," Martha offered. "You can take turns washing before we eat."

Martha took the girls under her wing and treated them as if they were her own precious granddaughters. After they washed up, the girls busied themselves by helping Martha set the table and dish up the food. "Were you planning on an army?" asked Dawn.

Martha chuckled and replied, "No, just four hungry teenagers! Glad I fixed a lot since there are five of you!"

As they sat down for breakfast, Charlie wouldn't let them eat before blessing the food. He told them he had been a preacher man before being assigned to the school's janitor position. Conversation was light as they passed the food, and all ate massive quantities. Aaron thought he would have to have another nap before he could do anything else!

Once they were sufficiently full, Charlie began to fill in some of the blanks regarding why their country was falling into chaos that would lead to communism if it wasn't stopped. "It all started sixty to eighty years ago. We dragged our feet getting involved in World War II because we didn't want to believe the horrific stories about Hitler and the Nazis. Japan did the world a favor when they attacked Pearl Harbor because it forced us to get involved. The goal of the Third Reich was world domination, just like they're trying to implement today. It's been called the fourth Industrial Revolution but in reality, it's the Fourth Reich. The people pushing for a one-world government are using Hitler's playbook, *Mein Kampf*."

"That can't be true!" exclaimed Dawn. Carly nodded in agreement. But Juan thought this made so much sense, especially as he thought about what his family uncovered about the coup being attempted on the United States. He shared his information, confirming Charlie's theory.

Charlie continued, "When they removed prayer from schools, legalized the killing of unborn babies, and started encroaching on parental rights, the family unit fell apart.

CHAPTER SIX

That's what they wanted. It's easier to control people if they have no hope for their future. What brings hope to a family? Their kids! Not allowing people to worship their God also diminished any hope for the future. If we are to survive as a nation, it's essential we get back to the biblical principles our founding forefathers used to write our Constitution and the Bill of Rights. People are created in the image of God, but we are all different, by design. God, in His infinite wisdom, didn't want us all the same. He wanted variety. We may be created in His image, but He also gave each of us specific talents and desires. I bet you're all different in what you want in life."

"That's so true! Exclaimed Dawn. "My brother is an avid outdoorsman, but I'd rather sing and find the music in my world."

"Perfect example, Dawn. You're brother and sister, alike in many ways, but still different." Charlie loved seeing the kids start to understand what their future could be like if they allowed God to show them what He intended for them. He also began to understand why the elites were targeting kids. If they could squelch the desires, the hopes and dreams of the youth, their plan for a one-world government would be all but achieved.

"What's your game plan on getting home?" Charlie asked.

They all sat quietly looking at each other, not knowing how much to say. Conner spoke up first. "Well, we really don't have a plan except to keep moving north as quickly and quietly as possible."

Martha was the next to speak up. "Well, that's a start. First things first, We need to change your appearance."

"That's what I said!" Carly exclaimed.

"Good!" Martha continued. "They're looking for two boys and two girls. We can cut your hair, girls. Short, change the color and dress you differently so that you look like a group of five boys. This will also add protection to you, girls. There are evil people out there who will want to do unspeakable things to your body if you get my drift. Aaron, I love your hair, but that carrot top is way too conspicuous. We're going to change your hair color too. You have a good start on what you picked up at the school. I'll help you pack it properly so you can carry it long distances, and we can add some things to your packs."

"Why are you doing this for us?" Conner was the first to ask the question they were all thinking.

"Because the majority has been silent for too long," Charlie started. "If we are to survive as the United States living under our Constitution, written to protect our republic, we should be required to allow the young people the same opportunities we had as youth. You are our future. It's a bright future if you are given the freedom to blossom as we did. If your generation takes the responsibility that comes with such freedoms, we will be successful again as the greatest nation this world has ever seen." Charlie let the truths of what he was saying sink in a bit before continuing.

"This is the only country in the history of the world that put the people above the government. Our Declaration of Independence, our Constitution, and the subsequent Bill of Rights were written by our founding forefathers in a time that was just as perilous as today is. I don't care what anyone says, those documents that formed our government were inspired by the true Word of God. We are a country that was founded on biblical, Christian values. They truly wanted to restrain the government, to give the people the power. It's been called the great American Experiment. If you're a student of history, you know the United States has become the wealthiest nation in the history of forever in the shortest amount of time. The experiment worked! The system works."

The kids were in awe of their newfound friends. Their reality was shocking yet exhilarating because they recognized the truth when they heard it. People would rather live free than enslaved. For too long the government had slowly been enslaving Americans with its regulations and directives. Selling peace and security in lieu of freedom. With the help of the media, the men and women in control sold the American people on the idea that they needed security to enhance their freedoms. They put their freedoms up as collateral for the security promised. As time passed, their guaranteed freedoms were sacrificed for a security that was never fully realized. More was always necessary to achieve the security that was supposed to ensure their freedoms. Both were mythical ideas, and both were being stolen from the people. People had to have the freedom to reach their personal dreams. Security would come with the freedom that wealth from a capitalist system produced. They were starting to see the bigger picture and why it was so important they get home to help revitalize the country. A silent revolution had been waging war on their country. It was time to stop it and get back to the basics. It was time to restore America.

Chapter Seven

Aaron wasn't too sure of his new hair color. He hoped the others wouldn't tease him too bad. He looked like a California beach bum with his golden locks of hair. The girls, however, underwent much greater changes in their appearances. Carly looked like a tough kid you wouldn't want to mess with in a dark alley. She would now go by the name of Carl. Dawn looked just like her brother now, only with darker hair than his. At least she would still be able to use her name of Dawn but would have to get used to spelling it as Don. Martha encouraged the boys to let their facial hair grow if they could. It would make them look older and hide their identity.

The book bags they had taken from the school were going to be returned in the morning. They now sported backpacks used by serious hikers. They were able to pack much more, and the weight was distributed better, so they could carry it further without much effort.

Charlie had supplied them with a small cook stove that folded down into a small box. A lantern was added to one of the packs in addition to a couple of sleeping bags and hammocks. Martha also insisted they take her last can of bug spray. She would find some more soon, she reassured them. She also bolstered their food supplies. Probably the most important addition to their packs was a water purifying system no bigger than a small knapsack, so they could make their own safe drinking water.

"Alright, kids, listen up," Charlie had them gather for what Conner thought was sure to be a "fatherly" talk. "You're about to get on board the revived Underground Railway. Do you remember studying about it during our Civil War in the mid 1800s?"

"Kind of. Did it have to do with freeing the slaves?" asked Conner.

"Yes, it did. The founding forefathers knew that sooner or later, slavery would have to be abolished. It wasn't how God intended man to live. We are all created equal in His image. However, today we are in certain ways all enslaved to our government's move to communism, so we felt it appropriate to emulate what our ancestors did when they fought to save this country from splitting apart and abolished slavery."

"Did you say we?" asked Aaron.

Charlie grinned at his new hair color. "Yes, I did. There is an entire network out there that will help you get all the way home. And we are ready to fight to save this country. Conner, your dad will be a valuable asset to our cause, so it's imperative you get to him and explain everything. You must convince him to join our cause."

CHAPTER SEVEN

"You know my dad?"

"Not personally, but I've heard about his courage and his willingness to make sure his men survived, and his heroism in the face of true evil while serving in the Middle East wars."

"Wow, he doesn't talk about what happened, and he really downplays his Congressional Medal of Honor. I'd really love to hear what he did."

"That's a story for another day, son. Maybe he'll share it with you someday. It'd be better coming from him anyway."

"Well, I don't think it will be too hard to convince him to help because I think he's sensing a lot of the problems you've explained to us. The hard part is going to be getting home."

"That's where our network of freedom fighters come in. We're everywhere and nowhere! Each stop is going to give you a password for the next stop. If you don't have it, you will never know they're a part of our group. For instance, when you get to where I'm going to send you, you must ask them about their son in Colorado. If they tell you he's about to be a daddy again, everything is fine. If they tell you they haven't heard from him or that they don't have a son in Colorado, you either have the wrong person or something is wrong. If they really don't know what you're talking about, you have the wrong people. Keep looking. If they drop a clue, you need to leave as soon as possible because they're somehow compromised.

They will indirectly let you know where the next stop is in their conversation, so pay attention."

"How will we know what the clue is?" asked Dawn. She was afraid they would miss the clue and they'd be on their own.

"Pay attention! It might be in something they say or something they do. I saw the message you sent to your parents. That was brilliant, by the way. That is what confirmed my suspicions of who you were when I saw you in my school. It will be like that. I know you can figure it out because you came up with that message for your families. Our network knows you're on the move."

"How do they know that? Does the government know where we're at?" Carly asked.

"We know from the back rooms on the web. You picked a great site to post in, Aaron. Keep looking there for information. The government knows you made it across the border. They're not sure where you're at, but they assume you're still in Texas. Right now, they're searching San Antonio. You were smart to get off the train before you got there. They also figure you'll be trying to get home. So we will probably send you the long way back. If someone wants to send you through Oklahoma, don't go. They're either compromised and sending you a message or they're not from our group and they want to assist in your capture thinking they'll get a reward. They'll be searching the most direct routes through Texas and Oklahoma. Aaron, you can't contact your brother Danny at OSU. They already have him under surveillance."

"Man, how do you know all this, Charlie?"

"You'll soon see we aren't small in numbers. In fact, your brother is a part of our group, and he was the one who told us about the group that has stakeouts on him 24/7, which confirmed it in his mind that you were okay. He also told us that your dad is aware of your safety and movements."

"Another thing to worry about is how the government will try to track you. Only turn on the cell phones that you have when you must make a call or check something on the web. Don't check the site you posted on from any of the phones that you use—only use computers to check there. Your identity can be obscured better from a computer versus a cell phone. Once you've used a phone one time, destroy it. Never use the same one twice and never travel with your phones on."

"Last topic. Have any of you ever used a gun?" Martha asked.

Conner spoke first saying that he was a pretty good hunter using a gun or bow. His dad taught him before the guns were confiscated, though they still had a couple that were hidden during the confiscation raids. "How do you happen to have a gun, Charlie? I thought most were collected several years ago."

"You'd be surprised at how many guns weren't registered, so they weren't collected. Plus, some guys have become efficient gunsmiths and make their own. We all pack our own powder to make our bullets."

He got up and slid the freezer in the living room to the side. There looked to be a trapdoor underneath that revealed a small arsenal of weapons. "Take your pick, Conner."

Conner chose an AR-15. His dad had one just like it that Conner used to shoot a deer a couple of years ago. Charlie agreed that while the AR-15 was a good weapon, it would be better if he took a handgun. It would be easier to conceal as they traveled. He offered him a Beretta that had a holster to conceal the gun in the small of his back. Juan had his eye on a hunting knife and crossbow with a quiver of arrows. Charlie told him to take them if he wanted. They would be good for hunting food as they traveled.

After a lunch of grilled cheese sandwiches, fresh cucumber salad, and a peach pie, Martha insisted they all take a nap because they would be leaving once the sun went down to travel at night.

Adam arrived at the school just as a hoard of media people were arriving. He ran as fast as he could to get inside before he was cornered by any of them. Principal Davis saw him coming and held the door for him and quickly closed it behind him.

"Thanks. I just can't talk to any of them right now!" Adam explained.

CHAPTER SEVEN

"I don't blame you. We just heard the news in the office. I'm so sorry for your loss. I guess you're here to pick up Evan?"

"Yes. Does he know?" He hoped not. He wanted to be the one to tell him. He knew he was going to have to withhold the good news from him until they got home. Evan would have to play the part as a grieving brother.

"No, not yet. I figured one of you would be here shortly. I don't envy you at all having to tell him about this. Let me have him sent to my office. It will give you the privacy you need. Take all the time you need."

"Thanks." Adam couldn't get anything else out. He wanted to seem grief-stricken, and yet he was busting with jubilation. He followed the principal into the office and allowed him to shut the door. He heard the page over the intercom for Evan to come to the office. He couldn't help grinning because he knew Evan would be wondering what he did to be in trouble. He noticed more media trucks arriving. What vultures! Did they think they would get a scoop from a kid who was only nine years old? Adam called Beth at home to see if the media was starting to gather there too. As the phone rang, he was glad they had already planned to get out of town today.

"Hi, Adam," Beth answered on the second ring. "I bet you're calling about the media swarm. Are they at the school too?"

"Hey, honey. Yes, they're here too. I was hoping they weren't at the house yet. We need to figure how to get out of town without anyone following us. We need to get away to figure things out."

"Do you have Evan yet?"

"No, he's on his way to the office. Principal Davis has given me the use of his office to tell him."

"Good luck, Hon."

"Thanks. Go ahead and get the car packed. It's in the garage, so no one will see you loading it. It should have a full tank of gas, so if we can figure a way to dodge the press, we can leave when we get back home."

"Adam, we need a distraction for me to leave. Do you think someone could help you guys leave the school undetected? Then we could get a message to the media that we're all at the school. The ones here should go there. That way I can leave and pick you guys up somewhere."

Just then, the school lunch truck pulled into the side drive, trying to make its way to the side entrance by the cafeteria.

"Good thinking! I know what to do on this end. Meet us at the school bus barn." As he hung up, the door opened to allow a scared Evan to walk in.

"Hey, buddy."

"What's going on, Dad? Why are all the media outside? All the teachers are giving me funny looks."

"Evan, there's been a story released to the media that says Conner, Dawn, Aaron, and Carly have been killed by the drug cartels." Adam tried to reach out to hug Evan, but he just pushed his dad away.

CHAPTER SEVEN

"No! It can't be true! You said they would be okay and that they'd be home soon!" He started to cry. He didn't know what to do.

Adam grabbed him up in a huge bear hug as Evan started to sob. "Let it out, Evan. Everything is going to be okay."

Evan tried to push his dad away. "How can you say that? They're dead! You promised they'd be home soon!"

Adam hugged Evan tighter. "Do you trust me, Evan?" he whispered in his ear.

Evan shook his head yes but kept crying. The tears wouldn't stop. He had bottled his feelings up for the past week ever since the nightmare started to unfold. His dad eased him to the couch and kept him in a bear hug, allowing him to cry.

Adam saw the principal shut the door. *Wow, that was quite a performance*, thought Adam. *That's good*! After what seemed like an eternity, Evan's crying turned to soft sobs.

"Evan, listen carefully." Adam was whispering so that no one or nothing could hear him except for Evan. "We are going to get out of here. I'm sure Principal Davis will help us leave on the school's cafeteria truck so that the media won't see us. We're going to meet Mom and head out to Granny's. I love you. I have so much more to tell you, but I can't right now. Trust me. We're going to be okay. We're going to take care of our ABC's."

Evan looked up at his dad. How could he be so calm? What was he not telling him? How could his dad be so cold, uncaring?

Adam wiped away his son's tears and kissed him on the forehead. "Ready, Evan?"

"I want Mom," Evan sobbed.

"I don't blame you, buddy." Adam feared Evan might be slipping into a state of shock. He had to get him out of here fast. Evan needed to share in the hope that he had. He needed to know the truth. He got up and asked the principal to come in. Evan sat on the couch, quietly crying as the two men talked. Adam came over and picked him up, telling him they were going home. All eyes in the school were on them as they passed through the hallway. Evan buried his head in his dad's shoulder trying to block everything out, the stares, the news, the nightmare that just wouldn't stop.

The bus barn was on the outskirts of town secluded from the highway by a large meadow. As Adam and Evan got out of the truck, Beth was pulling in. "Did you have any trouble leaving the house?" Adam asked her as she got out of the car.

Her answer was a short no as she ran to Evan and swooped him up in her arms.

"Mommy!" Evan's tears started all over again when he saw her.

"It's okay, baby! We're okay! I love you!" She kissed him repeatedly as she wiped away his tears, hugging him tight.

CHAPTER SEVEN

Adam thanked the truck driver and told him he appreciated his willingness to help them escape the barrage of media outlets. They weren't ready yet to talk to the press.

"I understand, sir. You take care of your family. Get out of here!"

They left town quietly, using back roads so as not to be spotted. Once they were safely out of town, Adam pulled the car over. He had to ease Evan's pain. He had to tell him the truth.

After his conversation with Adam, Aaron's father had gone back home and packed a bag as well. He had the same idea that Adam had. He was already in Oklahoma before the media swarmed the school looking for a story in Evan. Carly's parents weren't so lucky. They had no place to go. After a short interview in which they asked for privacy as they mourned the loss of their daughter, they went back in their home and closed the curtains to block out the circus in their front yard. They didn't have the luxury of knowing the truth.

The kids awoke to the smell of the grill cooking something that was sure to be wonderful. Carly and Dawn were the first ones to enter the kitchen to help Martha. She had hamburgers and hot dogs grilling by the back door with a huge bowl of potato salad chilling in the fridge. The girls helped her get the condiments ready while she pulled out a dish of baked beans from the oven. Dawn was sure they were going to miss her cooking when they left. Every meal reminded her of her granny's cooking. Large quantities were a must with tried-and-true family recipes that always tasted wonderful. She noticed a batch of homemade chocolate chip cookies sitting on the counter.

The boys emerged one by one claiming that they were starving. Martha chased them from the kitchen before they devoured half of the cookies. She sent them to the barn, where Charlie was preparing something for the kids' departure.

"Can you drive, Conner?" Charlie asked.

"Well, I have my license, but I haven't driven much. We never had the gas to just go for a drive." He responded.

Charlie was working on an old Chevy pickup. Half of the pickup bed had an extra fuel tank. He had converted the truck to run on propane since gasoline was in such short supply. "Might have to let you drive a bit tonight then to get some experience. You're going to go about 250 miles north and west to a small air strip just outside of San Angelo by the Twin Butte Reservoir. I'll go with you most of the way. But I need to drop you off and get back home before daybreak. No one must know that I've left town."

As he closed the hood to the engine he asked, "Do you remember the question for tonight's rendezvous?"

CHAPTER SEVEN

"Yeah, we're to ask if their son in Colorado has had their baby." Aaron responded.

"Close, but not quite right. Just ask him how his son in Colorado is doing. If he responds that his son is about to be a daddy again, everything is all right. You must ask the right question; otherwise, he'll think you're compromised, and he won't give you the right answer. If you ask the right question and *he* answers with a different answer, he's the one that's compromised. Understand?"

"Yes, sir," the boys responded in chorus.

"Good. Now start putting your stuff in the back. After supper when the sun goes down, we're gonna push Betsy down the road a bit. Don't want the neighbors to hear her." Charlie looked out toward the western horizon. "It's going to be a nice night for a drive, boys!"

Before they left, Charlie helped Aaron post another message. This one was very short. All it said was "Apples, Boys chasing Cats."

Chapter Eight

Granny was so thankful to see her family pull up in the driveway. The news on TV had been so heartbreaking. She ran out to greet them and immediately grabbed Evan and hugged him tight.

"I…can't…breathe…Granny!"

She didn't care. She spun him around and kissed him several times before putting him down. Adam was the next to be greeted by Granny. He turned the tables on her though by picking her up and spinning!

"Oh my," she squealed. "What do you know that I don't?"

Beth hugged her next and told her the good news about the kids. They couldn't contain their joy anymore, and it just spilled out as they jumped for joy and danced around with Granny in her yard.

"Come on in, and tell me everything!"

Granny busied herself fixing a light meal as Beth filled her in. Adam turned on her computer. He wanted to check out the website where Tom found the message. It was a sleazy site, but it did have some interesting posts on it.

CHAPTER EIGHT

When Evan asked him about some of the pictures, Adam got embarrassed. He didn't know Evan was looking too.

"Oh man, I didn't mean for you to see that garbage, Evan." He closed the laptop to block the pictures. "This is the site that Tom, Aaron's dad, found the message from the kids on. I'm sure they figured to get a message to us they would have to post on a website that the government wouldn't monitor very close. Can you do me a favor and go get our suitcases out of the car? If I find another message, I'll show it to you, but I don't want you looking at the other filth on here. Okay?"

"Promise me you'll show it to me?'

"Promise, buddy."

Evan shrugged and agreed to go get the luggage.

Adam opened the laptop as Evan left and started searching. Once you blocked out the filth, there really was a lot of information on the site. People found a way to communicate without the government monitoring them. After all, free speech was a right protected in the country's Bill of Rights written by James Madison. The founding forefathers understood that God-given rights had to be protected. In fact, they saw the freedom of religion and free speech to be such important rights that they were the first ones they deemed protected by our Constitution. Adam was beginning to realize that the current administration and subsequent government was not following the original Constitution. They had co-opted it and changed it to mean something that was not intended by the original framers of our founding documents. After serving his country proudly as a US Marine, he was beginning to become disillusioned in the course their once great country seemed to be on. He took an oath to protect this great country from all enemies, foreign and domestic. He just never figured he'd have to protect it from a domestic foe. The best thing about this website was realizing he was not alone in his thinking.

Just as Granny called out that it was ready to eat, he saw it! "Apples, Boys chasing Cats." He picked up on the ABC's, the reference to the family motto to take care of each other. He knew it was from Conner. They were moving again. "Evan! Come, quick!"

It had been a dusty ride in the back of the pickup, but altogether uneventful. Charlie had stayed on back roads as much as possible, and he allowed both Conner and Aaron an opportunity to drive a bit. Juan wanted a turn, but since he had never driven before, Charlie wouldn't let him try. He reasoned with him that they didn't have the time to teach him from scratch. There was almost a full moon, so Charlie had them drive without headlights as much as possible. He didn't want to draw attention to their journey if he could avoid it.

They pulled into what looked like a camping area and came to a stop by the reservoir.

CHAPTER EIGHT

"Okay, kids. Everybody out." They gathered their belongings as they stretched their legs.

"Where's the air strip, Charlie?" Juan asked.

"It's about fourteen miles ahead on the other side of the reservoir. Just follow the bank of the lake, and you'll eventually see it. Be careful because there will probably be people camping around here. Most are homeless and harmless. But there will be a sordid group wherever you go. Remember all those zombie shows that were popular several years ago?" Dawn thought that was a silly question but agreed with the others that she remembered. Their parents wouldn't let them watch the series, but their friends filled them in on the show, and she did see it several times while at friends' houses.

"Well, the people in charge did a really good job at making people dependent on the government programs. When our economy tanked and the money started running out, those people who had grown to depend on the handouts don't know how to fend for themselves. They've been trained to be takers because they were never taught how to take care of themselves. We legalized so many different drugs that were readily available, it kept the masses controllable. Plus, the drug cartels have a plethora of illegal drugs just as easy to access. They became zombies, drugged up, wandering around, looking for the next victim that they could attack and take whatever they wanted. These people usually congregate in the cities because there's more opportunities for them to take what they want from others. But some do roam the countryside. They're takers. They're mean. They think they're entitled to whatever you have because that is what they've been taught. Avoid them at all costs if possible."

"I'm afraid you won't be able to get around the reservoir before sunrise, so your best bet is going to be to camp here for the rest of the night and tomorrow. It's best to travel under the cover of darkness. There's a box canyon a couple hundred yards ahead. That will probably be the best place to hole up for the day. Try not to light a fire or cook anything. That will just draw people you don't want to mess with. Martha packed enough food items to eat that won't need cooked. The sleeping bags you're carrying are rated for below zero temps, so hunker down for warmth the rest of the night. Tomorrow, stay quiet and hidden. As soon as it's dark, head out for the air strip."

"Well, I'm officially scared now," Dawn commented.

"Me too," chimed in Carly.

"I don't mean to scare you. I'm trying to prepare you so that you can make it home, where you belong." Charlie gave the girls a big bear hug trying to comfort them.

"As bad as things seem, remember, the good always win. Battles can be lost to evil, but the war has already been won. I've read the Good Book. God wins!"

Juan thought that was a strange comment. He saw evil win plenty of times. He thought it was doing a good job at winning right now. They were on the run, hiding, trying

CHAPTER EIGHT

to avoid getting caught and killed. He thought Charlie was going senile in his old age.

Conner and Dawn understood and grinned. They both needed that reassurance.

"Well, guys, I'm an old preacher man, so I can't let you go without saying a prayer for you."

His prayer comforted the kids, calmed them, and gave them inner strength. Even Juan felt assured of the situation they were in, which he thought was strange. Hugs were given, and Charlie got back into Betsy and was gone.

Once he was gone, it grew eerily quiet. Aaron looked to Conner and asked, "Now what?"

"Let's find that box canyon and get hunkered down and out of sight. It's probably around two or three in the morning, so we should be able to get situated before the sun comes up." Conner took the lead, and the others quietly followed.

They almost missed the entrance to the canyon because of the overgrowth of shrubs and small trees. But once inside, it was the perfect spot to hide just as Charlie promised. Conner took the lead again, "Girls, find the spots you want to bed down in, and see what we can eat tomorrow. Be as quiet as possible. And no flashlights. We don't want to draw attention to ourselves."

"Aaron, how about we go back and make sure we didn't leave a trail coming in here?" Juan suggested.

"Good idea, guys!" Conner was glad they were thinking so strategically. "I'll stay here with the girls and get things set up for our security."

After a short hour, the girls were hunkered down and already fast asleep. Conner waited for the guys to come back. He thought they should take turns being on guard. Once the others came back, they agreed on Aaron taking the first watch.

They were thankful for an uneventful evening as they watched the sunrise. Breakfast consisted of hard-boiled eggs, jerky strips, and apples. It was hard to stay quiet but occasionally, they could hear voices—zombies wandering around looking for food or drugs, something to steal, or someone to harass.

"I'll take first watch this morning," Conner volunteered. "If I think our hiding place is about to be compromised, I'll lead them away from here."

"Do you think that's such a good idea?" Dawn was worried.

"I think two people should go on lookout. Safety in numbers," Juan suggested.

"I like that idea," Carly said. "But you need to let me and Dawn help with this too. We all need to get some rest also since we're traveling tonight."

Conner was reluctant to allow the girls to help, but he also knew five would be better than three. He asked Dawn to join him in the first shift. His ulterior motive

CHAPTER EIGHT

was to keep an eye on her; *always take care of your ABC's*, he thought.

As they took off to find good advantage points to post a lookout, Dawn winked at her brother. "Watching over your ABC's? I like it! But that is a two-way street, mister!" She motioned with her hand that she was watching over him too.

Conner grinned. She could be so annoying at times, but he really did love her.

They all heard several people while on watch throughout the day, but all in all, it was an uneventful day. They all got a good nap in and thus felt well rested. Martha didn't disappoint with the goodies she packed for them. They waited for several hours after the sun went down to start their journey around the lake. Their theory was that the zombies would get stoned or drunk and pass out after several hours of partying in the early evening.

I'd like to be in eyesight of the air strip before the sun comes up. Let's try to walk single file and be as quiet as possible. Don't want to wake up any zombies." Conner was grinning at his joke thinking it would lighten the mood.

The girls both punched him, not enjoying his humor at all. Juan giggled and said he'd take point and started walking. Conner followed with the girls trailing closely behind. Aaron took one last look around to make sure they were truly alone and then brought up the rear.

They had been walking for a while when Juan suddenly stopped and squatted down. As the others caught up to him, they crouched down beside him. Up ahead was the faint glow of a campfire. It looked like there were at least two people sleeping around the fire pit.

"Juan, check it out. See if we can circle around them without losing sight of the water and not disturb them," Conner instructed. As Aaron caught up with the group he added, "Aaron, go with him."

The boys moved out silently. If you strained, you could see where they were, but if you weren't looking, you wouldn't see them. Dawn and Carly soon lost sight of them entirely. It seemed like an eternity, but it wasn't more than five minutes. They saw someone approaching them from the same way the boys went. Conner hoped they were hidden enough to not be seen. He let out a sigh of relief when he realized it was Aaron.

He crouched beside Conner and pointed to a spot by the water about forty feet in front of them. "See that large rock by the water?"

"Yes."

"That's where Juan is waiting for us. I'm pretty sure it's only the three of them down there by the fire. One is snoring pretty loud, and there's a lot of empty beer bottles, so we think they're passed out drunk. Wouldn't want to wake them and find out though."

"Me either," agreed Conner. "Lead the way, Aaron. Girls follow his path exactly and be very quiet. I'll be right behind you."

CHAPTER EIGHT

The kids quickly made their way around the camp sight. Carly stumbled on a hidden tree root. They all stopped dead in their tracks as one of the guys stirred. He tried to sit up and look around but soon fell back down as he passed out again. Once they were all reunited with Juan on the other side, they kept going. Aaron kept glancing behind them to make sure they weren't being followed. He hoped their contact guy was there. He didn't want those zombies to wake up in the morning and start a scavenger hunt.

The rest of their hike was uneventful. They came up to the airstrip and did a quick search of the hangars. Everything was locked up tight. They found a spot hidden between a couple of the hangars to wait for sunrise and hopefully their contact. Carly pulled out some cooked bacon and biscuits along with some grape juice to share with everyone. As they settled in, the eastern horizon started to lighten up a bit. It was going to be a typical early summer day in Texas: hot and muggy. The girls nodded off as the boys kept watch in all directions for any movement, either from the zombies or from a possible contact to the underground railway.

It was peaceful at Granny's farm. Adam sat in the backyard watching the sun set as the chickens in the coop started to settle in for the evening. Evan was playing with Goober, the family dog, half Labrador, and half who-knows-what. His dad would have called him a mutt, but Granny insisted

Goober was more lab than anything else. He was a good companion for her. Smart, playful, and yet a fierce guard dog that Adam wouldn't want to mess with when he felt his owner was threatened. Granny and Beth were finishing up in the kitchen. It reminded Adam of a simpler time. This must be what his grandparents talked about. Reminiscing to an early time, life always seemed gentler, easier. Adam knew that wasn't exactly true. Life was constant. Usually hard with moments of pure happiness. History always had a way of repeating itself. *When would man learn from his past mistakes?* he wondered. Probably never. One could learn from their mistakes, but the lessons always seemed to get lost as the generations came and went. How many Sunday school stories was he told as a child that were centered on someone raising up in supremacy, ruling the masses, only to be beaten back into submission when the people had finally had enough? Heck, even his history classes at school were like that. Napoleon. Hitler. Mao. Countless others, always wanting and trying to rule the people instead of lead. He was sure the United States had become so powerful in such a short time because the founding forefathers put the people in control, not the government. It was established to help the people succeed. Unfortunately, the government had slowly co-opted the people's quest for freedom.

Now, their future seemed bleak. Communism was their new system of government, even though the powers that be claimed it wasn't. A silent coup had been transitioning the country to this oppressive form of government. One last massive push was probably coming to make the final transition. He reasoned this must be what the people thought and felt when Hitler and Nazism were on the rise. You could see the malicious actions of the Third Reich, and yet the news stories whitewashed it, tried to ignore it, thinking it would go away if you didn't react to it. "It wasn't our problem" was what most Americans thought before we were attacked at Pearl Harbor. But the world's silence emboldened the wicked ways of Hitler. It emboldened him to do more, take more. Hitler became drunk on the power he had accumulated. Others joined in wanting a piece of the accumulating dominance of a sick twisted man. *History is repeating itself, again*, Adam thought.

How do you defeat pure evil that seems to have all the power on their side? Trying to appease such evil never works, but that always seems to be the first choice of action people tend to take. Adam reasoned that it must be because most people aren't truly wicked. They will, however, take the road of least resistance. Power tends to corrupt how people think and act. Most men just want to live their lives in a way that provides for a decent living for their family and teach their children to do the same. "Raise your children in the ways of the Lord, and when they're old, they won't depart from it," Granny always said. Raise your children to do what's right. Raise them to let them go.

His thoughts turned to Conner and Dawn. He wondered what they were doing at this moment. Were they watching this beautiful night sky, enjoying a moment of calm in the midst of their storm? He hoped so. He wasn't ready to let his kids go. They weren't old enough. He was supposed to be there to protect them still. And yet, they were on their own.

He decided to try and get a message to the kids. If they were sending messages, they should be able to get one. *What can I say so they know it's me and yet keep us all safe?* he wondered.

Dawn and Carly woke up to what sounded like an angry confrontation. The boys were crouched behind some empty 55-gallon drums watching an older lady being harassed by the presumed zombies they passed last night. "She's feisty." Dawn whispered.

"We have to help her, guys," Carly added.

"What do you suggest?" asked Aaron.

"Well, we need a diversion so that you guys can get the jump on them. There are only three of them and five of us." Dawn thought her idea was solid. "I'll step out and taunt them. I bet they'll chase me, and I can draw them in here where you guys can get them."

"Then what? What do we do with them? What if that lady screams for help and others come and mistake us for the bad guys? I don't like this one bit!"

CHAPTER EIGHT

"We can't just let them do that to her, Juan! They're getting rough; they're going to hurt her!"

"Dawn's right," Conner agreed.

Wow, this was a dumb idea, thought Dawn as she stood up and started moving toward the commotion. As she approached them, she hollered out, "Hey, Granny, everything okay?"

The three turned their attention to her. "Son, this doesn't concern you. Turn around and go back to where you came from."

Son? What are they talking about? Dawn wondered. *Oh wait! My appearance transformation must be a good one,* she thought.

"No one treats my Grandma like that." She continued walking toward them, puffing out her chest and clinching her fists, pounding them together. She hoped she looked big and bad and not as stupid as she felt.

One of the zombies pushed the lady to the ground and then started coming toward Dawn as the others followed. "This is going to be fun, boys. We haven't had a fresh youngster for some time now. Stay with Granny, buddy." His words dripped with sarcasm. "I get first dibs on him!" The perceived leader was approaching fast.

Dawn stood her ground, she wanted to make sure they chased her, but she also wanted to make sure she got away. "You guys are idiots!"

She turned and ran as fast as she could. She heard his running footsteps closing in on her. Just as she was about to go in between the hangars, where the others were hiding, a gunshot rang out! She hit the ground and looked behind her. Her pursuer was lying face down, blood pooling by his head. The other two guys were running as fast as they could in the opposite direction. Granny was slowly picking herself up. *Where did that shot come from?* Dawn wondered. Did she just take them out of the frying pan and into the fire? The muzzle pulled back inside the window of the hangar on her right.

"Thank you, sonny. Are you all right?" The older woman was approaching Dawn.

"Yes, I'm fine, ma'am. Are you?" she asked as she stood up and started dusting herself off. She tried not to look at the body between her and the old woman, but she couldn't stop looking at it. "Is it normal for it to twitch like that?" she asked.

The lady couldn't help but laugh just as the hangar door opened showing the man who had made the shot. "You okay, Ma?"

"I'm fine Pa. Let's introduce ourselves properly to this young man who helped save me."

"I didn't do anything." Dawn didn't want any credit for what had just transpired even though it was her idea to interfere.

The older lady put her hand out and said, "I'm Virginia, and this is my husband, Paul. But our friends call us Ma and Pa."

CHAPTER EIGHT

Dawn shook her hand and paused for a slight moment before asking, "How's your son in Colorado doing?"

Dead silence. Knowing looks between the two. Dawn was beginning to think she just blew it big time. Ma wouldn't let her hand go. Her grip grew tighter. Dawn's fear spiked.

"Well, he's fine. About to be a daddy again. Thanks for asking," Pa said.

She let out a huge sigh of relief as Ma called for the others to come out now. Slowly, one by one, the others joined Dawn. They were slightly surprised when the other three came out of hiding. Aaron stayed hidden.

"Oh my, is that all of you?" Pa asked.

Conner took a defensive position between Pa and his sister. He should have never let her put herself in such danger. "Yes, this is our entire group."

"Did something happen to one of you? We were told to expect five." Ma was getting a worried look on her face.

"Come on out, Aaron," Dawn said. "I think we're safe with these guys."

"It's good to be cautious," Ma said, as Aaron came out.

"How did you know we were coming and that there were five of us?" asked Conner.

"Charlie told us, of course. We may be cautious and downright secretive when we meet people on the underground railway, but we do communicate frequently with our cohorts. Wouldn't want any passengers to fall by the wayside as they travel," explained Pa.

"What about those two guys that ran away? Do you think they'll be back?" asked Carly.

"I don't know. Maybe. We better bury this guy and clean up the mess. There are always sleazy people by the reservoir. They come out of the cities looking for food and drugs. They won't go to the police, but they might come back looking for revenge, so it's best to get rid of any evidence that they were ever here. Usually, they're so drunk or stoned, or both, to remember where they were or what happened," Pa explained.

The boys helped him bury the guy in between a couple of the hangars on the other side of the runway. Ma brought out a large water hose, and the girls helped her hose down the area and wash away the blood stains. Dawn felt sorry for him. Did he have any family? Why or how did he fall into such a state that he was a zombie, as Charlie called him? She was surprised about how callous she felt about all that had happened in the last couple of days. Gun shoot-out on the streets of Mexico and watching a man die there. Sneaking across the border and traveling incognito to get home. And now, another violent death of a man who was so messed up on drugs that he probably didn't know what he was doing half of the time. What was this world coming to?

They gathered in Ma and Pa's hangar shortly after the noon hour. "Now what?" asked Aaron.

"Well, first things first. Let's look to see if there are any pertinent messages out there for any of us."

CHAPTER EIGHT

Ma pulled out a tablet and they started searching the web. Slowly a plan began to develop as to their next move. Pa agreed that they couldn't go home through Oklahoma. He had a small plane that he would use to get them to their next stop. The question was: Where do they go next? The Internet was abuzz with news stories about an uprising of radical militants around the country. There was civil unrest everywhere. Demonstrations were getting violent in Atlanta over so many of the children dying from an unknown disease, like what the kids on the band trip had been exposed to. The government was starting to enforce lockdowns to supposedly stop the spread of this disease, but Pa thought they were trying to keep the masses in the dark to help subdue them and squelch the demonstrations. The camp where their friends from the trip had been taken to was quarantined. Everyone from their trip was being reported as dead. There were ongoing debates throughout the country on how to go in and clean up the camp without spreading the disease that was there. Did the place just need to be destroyed by fire to kill the virus that was there, or would it be a massive coverup of the truth of what really happened. News media outlets were reporting that the lockdowns nationwide could help to avoid a worldwide pandemic. California was fighting an ever-growing presence of the GIM terrorist group. They were getting bolder in their attacks and occupying portions of the state. The president was threatening martial law if the country didn't calm down and let the government do its job in protecting the people and providing for their every need. New York City had all but been shut down by riots lead by the unemployed. A group called Occupy Wall Street that had started years ago had been revived. They encouraged looting on a daily occurrence designed to shut down any business trying to make an honest living. The country seemed to be on a downward spiral that didn't appear to have a bottom or a way to stop the free fall into anarchy.

Just when they were all thoroughly depressed about the state of their once great country, they found a ray of hope. A message from home! Conner was sure it was from their dad! It said, "ABCDEfG,hijklmnopqrstuvwxy&z, now I know my ABC's next time won't you sing with me?" Conner was sure his family was at Granny's place, and they were all safe, for now.

Then they found another message! All it said was "Boomer, Sooners!" Aaron knew that his dad had gone to Oklahoma to be with his brother. Dawn felt sorry for Carly because there was no word from her family. Juan didn't have any messages either, but he didn't expect to get anything from his family. He wasn't even sure if any of them were alive.

Chapter Nine

Pa had been a pilot in the Air Force during the same wars that Conner's dad fought in. He now was allowed to use those skills as a crop duster pilot. He also maintained a Cessna plane that he used for carrying cargo or charter flights for some of the larger ranchers in Western Texas and politicians who wanted to look at the vast cattle ranges and crops to report to Washington, DC, what was still available for the food supply. The nation was getting hungry, and supplies were dwindling, so the big wigs had to put in their opinions on how to maintain and grow what was left all though most, if not all, of them had never raised any crops or handled cattle before. Most of the locals felt if they'd just leave them alone, they could get production up and work out their supply chain issues.

"Okay kids, let's get you to a safer place for the evening." Ma led the way around their two planes, through the back door of the hangar and down a narrow path to a small house not much better than a shack. It looked abandoned and almost ready to collapse.

"It's not much, I know, but it's been our home for forty-plus years," Ma explained. As they entered, it was clean and cozy. The whole house was open except for a small bathroom toward the rear of the shack. There was a curtain to one side that was halfway opened to show the bed for Ma and Pa. Toward the back was what could be considered the kitchen with some cabinets, a sink, a small refrigerator, and a cook stove. Carly felt claustrophobic with all of them in the tiny room. Ma opened a cabinet drawer, pulled out a false bottom, and pushed a hidden button. What had appeared to be a bookshelf in the front corner slid to the side and revealed a ladder descending into the darkness. Ma went first. At the bottom she turned on a light so that the kids could see the ladder and the open area that await them underneath. Pa was the last to come down, and he pulled a lever behind the steps that closed the entrance and moved the bookcase back so that it was hidden once again.

"That's cool!" Aaron said. When he turned to face the others, he saw an expansive room with sleeping cots on one side and storage racks on the other with any kind of survival gear you might need. Canned goods, camping gear, blankets, medical supplies, weapons, water, you name it; everything you might need was here. Toward the end was a small kitchenette with an upright freezer, a few cabinets, a sink, as well as a table and chairs. Also in the very back sat a desk with a computer and communication systems.

CHAPTER NINE

"Wow! I stand corrected. This is *very* cool!" Aaron exclaimed.

"Where did you get all this?" Juan asked.

"Oh, here and there" was the only explanation Pa would give.

"Make yourselves at home, kids. You'll probably be here for a day or two. Ma and I will stay upstairs. You'll be able to use our bathroom upstairs but only one at a time with permission. We don't want to raise any suspicions with the neighbors if they see too much activity here. Ma has a pork roast out back in the smoker that should be ready in about an hour."

The girls claimed two cots toward the back and were already looking through the toiletries provided by Charlie's wife to get cleaned up with. Aaron and Conner were drawn to the electronics in the back while Juan was looking through the supplies.

Pa joined Aaron and Conner. He pulled out a map to show the boys where they were at near the Twin Butte Reservoir by San Angelo, Texas. Another map of the United States was on the wall by the computer. Pa explained that all the highlighted areas were where the resistance was growing and how the underground railway was expanding.

"We can pull this up on my computer so that you can have a copy to take with you." Your dad will want to see it. He's very good with logistics from what I remember serving with him. He can formulate plans to help us fight this evil regime trying to takeover."

"You know my dad?" Conner asked.

"Oh yes! His tactics helped us to bring the conflicts in the Middle East wars to an acceptable end so that we could all come home. He more than earned that Medal of Honor although I'm sure he wouldn't agree."

"He never talks about what happened over there. Can you tell me?"

"Nope. That's a story your dad needs to tell." Conner thought it curious that Charlie had said pretty much the same thing about his dad. He missed him so much! He wanted to have that conversation with him, to find out more about him, to help him with the predicament the country was in now. He wanted to get back to a more normal life, especially for his younger brother Evan.

Pa was telling Aaron and Juan about an upcoming trip he was planning for Clovis, New Mexico. He was taking a load of fertilizer up there for some local farmers he knew. He'd be flying his bigger plane to accommodate the cargo. Depending on how heavy the load would be, and some additional planning, he thought the kids could ride along.

Several days had passed, and Beth thought Evan seemed to be settling in well with the new routine at Granny's. He enjoyed helping with the chickens and

CHAPTER NINE

planning the garden with Granny. Her garden spot was ready to plant, and they needed to get started. Evan liked being a part of something worthwhile. Even at his age, he felt the need to contribute. They never had the time or place for a garden back home in Wichita. She wondered if they'd ever get back to their home. Adam had discussed with her the possibility of going back for a few more of their things, but Adam wasn't sure how safe it would be for them there. They agreed they really needed more of the kids' clothes but were reluctant to go back. Adam had convinced his boss that with losing the oldest two kids, the family needed to stay put for a while at his mother's farm. He was able to work remotely for the time being, which seemed to satisfy the government's requirements for contributing to society. He knew he'd have to arrange a trip soon to check in at his employment and make sure the proper paperwork was in place for his remote work status, which would give him the excuse to go by their house and pick up some things. Beth's job could not be done remotely, but the company agreed Beth needed time to grieve for her children and help Evan adjust. The local grocery store offered a position to help keep the government satisfied that she was still contributing for the good of the people while she worked through her grief of losing two kids.

Adam kept searching the dark web for any new information on the kids. He was amazed at the ground swell of true patriots who hated what was happening to their beloved country. He was building a solid network of others across the land who eventually might become firm assets willing to do whatever it takes to reclaim America from the increasing sledgehammer of the oppressive regime. Never in a million years did Adam think he would have to fight communism in his own country. His war time experience fighting totalitarian regimes who used terrorism to scare people into compliance seemed to be a strong possibility of becoming very useful here.

Ma got the kids up early and had breakfast ready for them. Today was the day they were going to get a little bit closer to home. Pa had the plane prepped and loaded for their journey today.

Pa started their conversation with, "Let's review the itinerary for today. We're taking the company plane that is already fueled and has the fertilizer payload secured. You'll be riding in the very back behind a false panel I put in for occasions like this, out of sight, out of mind. When we land, I'll go in to show my paperwork and arrange for them to off-load me. Our contact there is one of the airport workers. He'll come on the plane and knock seven times on the false panel. His knock will be twice, then a pause, and five more rapid knocks. When you come out of the hold, what do you say?"

"Is this Denmark?" Conner said.

CHAPTER NINE

"Right, and what will his response be if it's safe to deplane?" Pa asked.

"Sure, if you came by way of London," Conner answered.

"That's a silly code! It doesn't make any sense!" Dawn chimed in.

"Well, it doesn't have to make sense now, does it?" Pa quipped. "You're just trying to determine if it's safe to get off the plane or not. If he says anything else besides the correct phrase, he'll close the false panel. I'll do the same knock as he did and open it up when it's safe to get you off."

The group finished their breakfast and retrieved their backpacks for the trip. Ma had replenished the food supplies for this leg of the journey. Pa gave them an iPad to communicate with if things weren't going as planned. It was safer than their phones, plus not as easy to trace. They were all ready to move on. Their stay in the hideout below Ma and Pa's shack was nice but claustrophobic after a couple of days, especially to Dawn. Pa gave them an extensive lesson on the underground railroad and the patriots who were connecting through the dark web. The drumbeats of war were getting louder. Conner wanted, no, needed to get home and talk with his dad about all that he'd learned on this trip. Aaron had devised the next message for their families and posted it last night on the same page as the last one. It simply said the pony express rides again.

Walking to the hangar was a quiet trek. Once in the hangar, Ma pulled them all in for big ole bear hugs. Carly and Dawn both fought back tears. Carly didn't know if it was because she'd miss Ma and Pa, fear of being on the move again, or acknowledging she was homesick and just needed to get home. Pa helped them into the hidden compartment he had rigged in the back of the plane. It was very small but sufficient for the two-hour flight. The biggest issue was that it would be dark once the false panel was in place. Dawn was afraid she would get very claustrophobic, sitting in the dark, not being able to see where they were.

"I'll sit by you, Dawn," her brother offered.

"I'm sure we'll all get a bit scared, but just think of how much closer we'll be to getting home and seeing our families." Aaron was trying to stay optimistic and calm everyone, including himself. He wasn't looking forward to getting in the hidey-hole either.

Adam sat down at the breakfast table with a big grin on his face.

"What?" Evan asked.

"The pony express rides again" was all he had to say.

Evan leaped for joy! He knew what that meant! His brother and sister were coming home!

CHAPTER NINE

The plane ride to Clovis was uneventful once their eyes adjusted to the dark. The humming of the plane's engines was relaxing. Both girls dozed off while the guys discussed what they'd do when they made it to Granny's home. Juan knew he couldn't go back home. He was almost certain his family had been murdered. Conner assured him he could stay with his family. Aaron wanted to get to Oklahoma to be with his dad and brother, but from what they were seeing on the web, it wasn't a safe option for him. The discussion turned to how to possibly get Aaron's family to Kansas. He hadn't received any messages back from his dad since the first one, which was concerning. He knew his brother was part of the underground resistance, so he knew they had to be seeing his posts. Were they under such tight surveillance that they couldn't respond? He hoped that was all that it was.

Pa was an excellent pilot, and their landing was as smooth as could be. He turned off the engines and went into the terminal. The kids sat quietly, anticipating the knock that was supposed to come. Soon they could tell the fertilizer cargo was being unloaded. Muffled voices, skidding of containers moving toward the door. But no knock. What was going on? It became quiet again. They assumed the cargo was off-loaded. Where was their contact? Where was Pa? Should they open the false panel and look outside? How long had it been since they landed?

"Why don't I take a look?" Juan asked.

"I'm not a part of your band group. They're not looking for me. I can speak Spanish and pretend I don't know English. If I'm caught, they'll think I'm just an illegal from Mexico. They'll take me in, give me a court date, and let me go. You know, catch and release. I have a better chance of finding out what's going on without raising suspicion."

Conner was the first to respond. "I don't like it, but I agree it's the best chance we have to find out what's going on. Try to be back in an hour. If you do get caught, once you're released you head to my Granny's place."

"Yeah, you're always welcome there," Dawn added.

They slowly opened the false panel. The sun was obviously getting lower in the western sky. No one was around the plane, and the cargo door was still open. As Juan looked out, he saw the fertilizer cargo sitting on pallets near the terminal, but no people were around. He let everyone know what he was seeing and that he was going to head toward the terminal to see what he could find out. As he approached, the door opened and out walked Pa with another man. Juan ducked behind the pallets for cover. Pa had seen him, but the other man didn't thanks to Pa distracting him. The men shook hands and split up. Pa was headed toward the plane, but Juan didn't think he could get back without the other guy seeing him.

In the plane, Pa gave the agreed upon knock and slid open the false panel. "What the hell is Juan doing?" he yelled.

CHAPTER NINE

"We got scared and wanted to know what was happening. Juan thought he was the logical one to look around because if he was caught, he could pretend to be an illegal, which technically he is. He figured catch and release would be what happened to him," Carly explained. "Don't be mad at him or us! We knew something wasn't right, so we wanted to find out."

"Well, you're right. The plan has changed, but it's for the better. I leave in the morning headed to Dodge City, Kansas, to pick up some executives who need a ride back to Texas. Hopefully, Ma packed enough food to get you through the night. Was Juan planning on coming back to the plane soon?"

"Yeah." Conner told Pa that Juan was to only be gone about an hour.

"Hopefully, he can make it back. This place is crawling with added security and ICE agents. I'm sure they're looking for you guys, which is amazing since you've been reported as dead. I'm going to move the plane closer to the terminal off the runway. Maybe that will help Juan if we're closer to him." Pa closed the plane door and proceeded to taxi the plane to its parking spot for the night.

As nighttime settled in, it became eerily quiet. The darkness seemed oppressive, like it was sucking the air out of the plane. Clovis was a small enough airport that it closed for the evening. Hopefully that would help Juan to make it back in time for their departure in the morning. Ma did indeed pack enough for the kids to eat a decent meal. "I wonder where Juan is." Dawn wasn't really talking to anyone, just expressing what everyone was thinking. Did he see where the plane had been moved to? Would he, could he make it back before they left in the morning?

Aaron and Conner took turns throughout the night staying on watch for Juan and whoever else might be lurking around the plane. It was well after midnight when the boys heard someone enter the plane. They were hopeful it was Juan but knew that they had to be sure before opening the false panel. Whoever was out there seemed to be rummaging through the plane. Juan would have known to knock on the panel. No knock came. Muffled voices seemed to be talking about looking for any valuables that could be snatched. The English was broken and hard to understand and hear for that matter. Were these zombies, like what they ran into near San Antonio? ICE agents looking for them? Conner started praying that they wouldn't find their false panel.

"Look!" one of the intruders shouted. There's someone out there by the side door of the terminal. Let's get 'em!"

The intruders quickly left, and shouting could be heard in the distance. Conner wanted to open the panel to see what was happening but knew he'd better not. At least for a little while. What if they had left someone behind? Or if they were coming back? Who did they see? Juan? Another zombie? Border patrol agents? Dawn, who had also been awake, started to cry.

CHAPTER NINE

Conner quickly put his arm around her and motioned for her to be quiet. She buried her head on his shoulder and continued crying. Conner felt tears welling up in his eyes also, but he knew he had to stay strong for the group. As the evening grew quiet again, they both dozed off.

Chapter 10

After filing his flight plan, Pa went out and started his plane to taxi to the end of the runway. The motion woke the kids, but they kept quiet in their hiding place. As he sat at the end of the runway, waiting for clearance to take off, Pa went to the back and gave the secret knock on the false panel. Aaron opened the door. "Where's Juan?" he asked.

"I don't know" was Pa's reply. "I don't have a lot of time but wanted to assure you that we're headed to Dodge City, Kansas. I know Juan hasn't been captured by the ICE agents, but there was a lot of commotion last night with what everyone calls the zombies that scavenger for food and drugs anywhere they can. They often hit the airport early evenings looking through the newly arrived cargo. Hopefully Juan avoided them too. All we can do now is keep him in our prayers."

Dawn knew he was right, but she couldn't help but start crying again. How was he going to make it to Granny's home now? "Please, Lord, keep him safe," she quietly prayed.

Pa continued, "When we land, I'll knock on your panel. Wait five minutes, then come out. You'll see a shack that should be close to where I've parked the plane. Make your way there and wait inside till evening. I'll be long gone with my passengers heading back to Texas, so good luck on your next leg of your journey home.

"How will we know what to do next or who we can trust?" Conner asked the question they were all wondering.

"There will be a blue backpack left for you. If it's any other color, don't touch it. If the backpack is blue, you'll have instructions on what to do. If it's not blue, when it's dark, leave the shed and head north. Keep your eyes peeled in the ditches. You should come across the blue pack within a mile or two with help to get you home. If you don't see one, you're on your own to get there. I'd advise to travel at night only."

"I've specifically not asked you where you're Granny's farm is located because I want plausible deniability." Pa stopped. He looked troubled, almost like he could cry. "Kids, I'm sure you know by now, we are in a world of hurt. You've seen it up close and personal, firsthand. But the big picture is that our nation, our world, has turned its back on Jesus. He's such a loving, passionate God. He even sent his Son to take our penalty for our sins. But He's also a gentleman. Mankind has said they don't want Him, so it seems God has taken His hand of protection away. I'm not sure of our immediate future, but I know God is in control. We must pray for revival but plan for survival. Ma and I will continue to pray for safe travels for you." With that, Pa closed the door as they heard the tower give him clearance to take off.

It was a cold night for this time of year in Clovis. Juan had found a place to hide from the ICE agents and the scavengers earlier in the evening. He had been trying to get back to the plane when he saw the agents board. He knew he had to cause a commotion to get them off the plane to save his friends. But what to do? Soon he saw a group of about five or six rummaging through cargo pallets sitting on the tarmac. Moving toward them, he shouted out in Spanish to get their attention and hopefully the agents would hear also. It worked! The agents on the plane were coming toward him, but so were the zombies. He decided to run toward them. As he got closer, they saw the agents chasing him. Juan caught up to them and yelled, "Run! Run!" Everyone scattered like rats leaving a sinking ship to get away from the agents. Two of the zombies were caught as they fell trying to get away. That slowed most of the agents down, but one kept coming. The apparent zombie leader told the group to split up. He pointed to Juan and told him to follow him. Juan complied. His first goal was to avoid capture and then figure out a way to get away from this group of vagrants. As they hit the tree line, Juan saw his chance to get away. As the group went left, he chose to go right. The path was overgrown and rocky, but

CHAPTER 10

he kept running. Soon he couldn't hear anyone chasing him. He turned to look and saw he was alone. Slowing to a fast walk to catch his breath, he started looking for a place to hide for a bit before trying to get back to the plane.

Juan woke to the sound of a plane taking off. As he looked back toward the airport, he saw that it was Pa's plane. His heart sank. Why did he allow himself to rest instead of heading back to the runway? Now what? He knew where he needed to go, Granny's farm in Kansas. But how would he get there? How can he find the underground railroad to help him? Or was he on his own?

It was a bumpy flight to Dodge City with a rough landing. Carly and Dawn were fighting air sickness and were anxious to get there and get off the plane. Excitement was growing also. They were almost home! So close to Granny's! And yet, so far. Conner figured they were still at least seventy-five miles from the farm.

The knock from Pa came as expected, so now they waited. Aaron commented that it was the longest five minutes ever, which everyone agreed with. Slowly, Conner opened the door, making sure no one was around. They saw the shack Pa spoke of about forty feet away.

"You go first, Aaron," Conner whispered. "Once inside, make sure it's safe, then I'll send the girls and follow as quickly as I can."

Aaron cautiously looked around and then made a mad dash to the door of the shack. He opened it quickly and disappeared inside. Soon he cracked open the door motioning for the girls to come. Conner made sure the false panel was in place before exiting the plane and closed the outer door also. He saw Pa out of the corner of his eye as he made his way to the shack. It looked like he was smiling as he entered the terminal. Conner was deeply thankful for all Pa had done for them and was going to miss him. He'd have to be sure to send a coded message when they were home safe to let all those who helped them know. Maybe he could find out what happened to Juan also and help him get to Granny's.

As he entered the shack, Aaron and the girls were all standing around a blue backpack, grinning, waiting for him before they opened it.

"Let's see what we got," said Conner as Aaron picked it up.

Inside were peanut butter sandwiches, water bottles, granola bars, and apples. "I'm starving!" Dawn squealed as they dug in.

A side pocket had a hand-drawn map and Kawasaki keys. "Looks like our next mode of transportation will be motorcycles or ATVs," Aaron speculated.

They ate as they studied the map. It looked like at the edge of the airport sat another small building where they should find their next mode of transportation. The instructions said they could take it as far as they needed, but

CHAPTER 10

when they were done, they needed to get it to Macksville and hide it in some bushes by the grain elevator.

"Dawn, that's about ten to twelve miles from Granny's! I remember taking wheat there with Grandpa years ago when we helped with harvest."

"I remember that also, Conner! We can be there sometime tomorrow!"

"Lord willing," he replied. "Let's take Pa's advice and travel at night. I think there's a full moon, so it should help us find the bikes and our last part of our journey home."

Carly had been sitting quietly, with a confused look on her face. She had never been to a church or heard anyone talk about God or pray. It hadn't been a priority in her family, and when they banned all churches except the Unified Brethren Church, it wasn't anything her family was interested in, so it wasn't missed. But she had witnessed an impossible journey made possible by strangers who were willing to risk everything to help them. All along the journey, starting with Juan, then Charlie in Devine, and Ma and Pa in San Angelo, they all seemed to have a faith in something or someone that she was unaware existed.

Dawn saw her confusion. "What's wrong, Carly?"

"I don't know." She knew she was tired—"exhausted" would be a better word for how she was feeling—but the confusion of the possibility of someone or something helping them was overwhelming.

"I know what's troubling you," Dawn started. "I felt it also. But it stirred up memories of when we were little, and we'd go to church before they were banned. We learned about God and how He loved us so much that He sent His Son to rescue us from ourselves. He provided a gift. All we have to do is accept it."

"How do you do that if you don't know what the gift is?"

"It's a gift, silly! Do you know what your gifts at Christmas or your birthday are before you open them? No. It's usually something we want or need. In this case, it's something we need. We've all messed up. We've all sinned. And when you look at our world, you see just how badly we've messed things up. God knew we'd mess up! He sent His Son, given to us at Christmas time. His Son's name is Jesus. And He spent His time on earth telling us about His Father and how much He loved us. Then, He took our penalty for our sins, He died for us! And the best part, He arose for us!"

"Is that what Easter is about? Or used to be about?" Carly asked.

"Yes! All you have to do is accept it! Just like at Christmas or your birthday. It's a gift for you, but if you don't accept it, it's technically not yours."

"How do you accept it?"

"Most people call it praying. I call it talking to God. Admit you've messed up. Ask Him to forgive you and accept His gift of eternal life."

"That's it?" Carly asked.

CHAPTER 10

"Yep, that's it!"

Carly sat quietly for a while, thinking about all Dawn had shared with her. Dawn had gone over to sit with Conner and Aaron as they discussed the next leg of their journey.

"Okay, Lord," Carly started quietly talking with God. "I'm a mess. You know it. I know it. Forgive me. I need and want You now in my life." She felt an amazing peace come over her. It was like a boulder had been lifted off her. She felt a smile form on her lips. She looked up at the others as they were watching her.

"Welcome to the family," Conner said as Dawn ran over to give her a big hug.

Adam had gone back to Wichita to confirm his paperwork to work remotely so all would be in place. It truly was a depressing trip, and he was glad that it could all be done in a day. After taking care of his paperwork, he went by their home. He was glad Beth didn't come with him. She would be devastated to see what now could only be called a house. Graffiti covered the front, including the garage door, and it looked as if someone had tried several times to break in. As he pulled up, neighbors stared at him. What could have persuaded the people who they considered friends to turn so quickly against them? He knew Aaron's dad was in Oklahoma with his older son and was aware that the kids were on their way home. He wanted to stop by Carly's folks to hopefully get them up to speed and attempt to alleviate some of their pain.

As he entered through the garage door, he remembered the package they had received before leaving and how Sharon, Sally's mom, prevented him from opening it. He wondered whether Carly's family had received one. He looked to see that the package was still hidden where he had left it. He wondered whether he should try to take it with him. He didn't want anyone to find it and open it. He also didn't want to take it with him but thought that he could dispose of it safely at the farm.

He gathered several suitcases of the kid's clothes and a couple of Beth's outfits. Evan had told him he would like some of his toys. He also grabbed some family pictures. He was pretty sure they'd never be coming back, and if they did, he didn't think it'd be very soon. Plus, who knew what shape the house would be in. Before he left, he went up into the attic and pulled his military duffle bag down. He opened it to confirm his weapons were still there. He wanted those to go with him. If he were caught with them, he'd be thrown in jail for illegally possessing firearms, but at this point, he figured if this cold war went hot, he wanted to at least be armed.

As he left the house, he looked up Carly's address. He pulled out of the driveway, and a neighbor approached his car. He looked almost as if he was drugged. He was menacingly coming at him swinging a baseball bat. At first,

CHAPTER 10

Adam wanted to talk with him to get some information about all that had been going on in the area but thought twice about it when he saw the glazed look and his twisted facial expression of anger. He floored his car, thankfully missing the man by inches.

The neighborhood Carly's family lived in wasn't far, and it looked as run down as his community. As he approached the address, he could see that the house had burned. An older woman was walking her dog, so Adam rolled down his window and slowed down to talk with her.

"Excuse me, ma'am. Can you tell me what happened here?"

She had a blank stare on her face. She looked at the house and then back at Adam.

"Have you seen my Carly?" she asked. "My house burned, but I can't find her."

Adam realized who the lady was and that she was in shock.

"Ma'am, I can take you to her if you want. Where's your husband?"

"He's in there," she said as she pointed to the house. "I can't move him because the second floor is on his head. Have you seen my Carly?"

Oh my! Adam had seen this reaction in the war when people were shell-shocked. He knew he had to take her with him, but he knew there could be horrific consequences if anyone found out that he took her. They'd probably accuse him of kidnapping. Or worse. But she needed help, and she wouldn't get it here.

"Ma'am, can I take you to Carly?"

She looked at him with a blank stare. She seemed hesitant probably because of the shock, plus she didn't know him. "What's your dog's name?" Adam thought if he could find some common ground, she'd be more willing to go with him.

"His name is Bob. Carly named him because he has a bob tail."

"Hello, Bob. Would you like to go see Carly?" The nub of his tail started to wiggle.

Then slowly she went around to the passenger side of the car and got in. "Have you seen my Carly?" she asked.

"Yes ma'am. Let's go see her." He didn't know what he was going to do until the kids showed up, if they showed up at all, but he knew he couldn't leave her behind.

Chapter 11

The kids left their hiding place about an hour after sunset. They had watched Pa leave mid-afternoon with his passengers headed back to Texas. Pa seemed to give a quick glance in their direction with a sly smile on his face. He knew they were safe and ready for the next leg of their journey home. He was ready to get back to Ma so they could rejoice together and pray for the kids and others out there that needed help. At the edge of the airport was the other small building with a Kawasaki UTV inside, just like the instructions had said.

"Let's wheel it outside and away from the building before we start it. Hopefully that won't draw as much attention." Aaron explained. They had decided to try and stay off the main highway as much as possible. Conner estimated it'd take them a couple of hours to reach Macksville. Conner was more familiar with the area since his grandparents lived nearby, so he volunteered to drive.

It was a beautiful evening, and the full moon made it easy to travel without their headlights. Dawn thought one could almost be tricked into thinking everything was back to normal, the way it was when they were younger and would come see Granny. She missed the good ole days! A giggle escaped her as she thought how ridiculous that sounded! She was barely a teenager, and she was reminiscing about the good ole days! She started humming one of her favorite songs. The night air was still warm with the wind blowing her hair backward. Her long hair was gone, but that was probably for the best. It helped disguise the fact that she was a girl, plus it had made it easier to take care of. She was beginning to think they might make it home. Oh, how she missed her mom! She missed her whole family.

"I haven't heard you sing since we were on the train," Conner said.

"Clickity clack, don't look back!" Everyone laughed at the little ditty she had made up on the train.

"It's kind of nice. Reminds me of the good ole days when I used to tease you about how bad you sounded!" Conner loved teasing his sister!

"Ha! I was just thinking about the good ole days too. It made me giggle because we're so young. How can we be reminiscing of days that weren't that long ago?" she wondered aloud.

"A lot has happened since the last president was inaugurated," Conner replied.

"You mean installed, don't you?" Aaron added.

"It sure seems like that's more accurate than 'inaugurated.' Can't wait to get home and talk to Dad about everything we've seen and learned. Wish Juan was still with us! He had a lot more details than me."

"I hope he's okay," Carly added. "He's smart. Hopefully, he'll figure out a way to get to your granny's place soon. Not to change the subject, but how will I get to Wichita to see my parents?" All rode in silence for a while. They knew they were incredibly lucky to be so close to Granny's but also knew they were not out of danger. No one was. Times had changed, and there seemed to be no going back to those good ole days. There was a new normal, and they didn't like it.

It was well after midnight, but the full moon made for a nice evening drive. Adam pulled onto the long driveway to Granny's house. Carly's mom had been asleep since leaving Wichita. He realized he didn't even know her name. He hoped she wouldn't freak out when she awoke. He had told her his name, but she was in such a state of shock that he wasn't sure it registered with her.

Out of the corner of his eye, he caught the movement of something, or someone, in the ditch. He kept going. Adam didn't want to take on another stranger with Carly's mom still in the car. He decided he'd walk back after getting her settled to see if he could determine what or who was lurking on their driveway.

Beth met him at the car when she noticed he had a passenger. "Who do you have?"

"It's Carly's mom, but I don't remember her name." He quickly explained how he had found her and knew he couldn't leave her behind. Beth opened the car door.

"Hello, Carla," Beth said, as she recognized Carly's mom. They had met at several of the girls' school functions. "Hi," she responded. "Do you know where my Carly is?"

Beth looked at Adam with a questioning look, not knowing how to answer Carla.

"She's on her way with her friend, Dawn, our daughter," Adam explained.

"Do you know when they'll be here? I need to tell her about her dad." That admission seemed to open the flood gates of tears and sobbing grief. Beth put her arms around her to comfort her and lead her into the house.

———◆———

The kids arrived at the elevators in Macksville and had hidden the UTV as instructed. They skirted around town and headed toward Granny's place. Conner thought it'd take them about another hour to walk the rest of the way. The closer they got, the more excited they became. Aaron was thankful they hadn't seen any other vehicles so no one would know where they were or where they were heading. He thought they might be making too much noise, but

CHAPTER 11

then, they seemed to be in the middle of nowhere with no one else around.

"Look, Conner! There's the driveway to Granny's!" Dawn squealed.

They all froze as they saw the car turn down the drive. Who would be going there in the middle of the night? They kept going in silence. Conner saw the movement first and then Aaron. "Girls, stay put until we figure out what's out there," Conner said.

They split up to see whether they could encircle whoever or whatever was hiding at the beginning of the driveway. The closer they got, the surer they were that it was a guy who was hiding, unsure of what to do next. Aaron came up behind him. Conner stood up in front of the guy to distract him as Aaron pounced on him from the rear, dropping him to the ground. Conner ran to help Aaron when they realized who it was. "Juan! How'd you get here?" Conner yelled as he gave him a huge bear hug.

The girls ran up as they realized what was happening and joined in the happy reunion.

"Man, am I glad to see you guys!" Juan said. "When I saw Pa's plane take off, I knew I had to find a different way to get here. There's a lot of people wandering around out there. Some are like us, caught up in circumstances beyond their control, trying to get some place safe. Others are like the zombies we saw at the lake. I distracted some ICE agents searching the plane at the airport by teaming up with some zombie-like characters but was able to ditch them. My heart sank when I saw Pa's plane take off and was mad at myself for falling asleep while hiding from that group of delinquents. I hitched a ride with some migrant workers headed north. They were so nice and so scared about what's going on. One of them knew my dad! But they also told me most of my family scattered before being attacked in our home. They don't think my parents made it, but my sisters crossed the border with them. They actually thought about going back to Mexico but found out the drug cartels have teamed up with your government. The border is going to be erased when we all become one country, but crossing back and forth will be harder for people not willing to go along with this new nation."

"I'm so sorry about your family, Juan!" Carly said. "I can't imagine how hard it must be to hear such horrific news and not know where your sisters are."

"Thanks. It's hard to comprehend." Fighting back tears, he wanted to be strong for their group. "But I have hope that my sisters are somewhere safe. Oh, and you'll never guess who was helping them!" Juan exclaimed.

"Who?" Carly and Dawn asked in unison.

"Charlie! That's how I knew they were safe to travel with! They're on their way to Nebraska to meet up with other family members. They dropped me off a couple of miles from here. From your description, Conner, I figured this had to be the drive to your Granny's place. I was waiting until morning to approach the house."

CHAPTER 11

Adam put the car in the garage and had Evan help unload the items he had picked up at home. He grabbed his pistol, loaded it, and put it in the small of his back under his shirt. "Evan, tell Mom I'll be back soon. Also, tell her to lock all the doors." Evan gave him a questioning look but quickly obeyed his father as Adam headed back down the drive. He cut into the tree row to hide his movement and moved as fast as he could while remaining as quiet as possible.

He heard the voices of several people. He slowed his approach. He wasn't sure how many were out here or whether they were armed or what their intentions were. He could tell there was a mix of men and women in the group ahead. They seemed to be happy and not very concerned about who or what else was out here. He continued to close in on the group.

"Guys, are you ready to go see Granny?" Conner asked.

"YES!" Dawn shouted.

Adam couldn't believe what he heard! The kids had made it! He stood up. He was right across the road from the kids. Juan saw him first and screamed. Conner turned to see what had scared him.

"Dad!" He took off running toward him only to have Dawn beat him to their dad's arms.

The others crossed the road also and stood around, laughing and rejoicing that they had made it. "Dad, we have so much to tell you! Oh, and this is Juan. He's the reason we made it out of Mexico," Conner explained.

"And the underground railroad got us home!" declared Dawn.

"Yes, we all have a lot to talk about but first things first. Let's go see Granny!"

Epilogue

What Happens When *After Life as We Know It* Becomes Reality?

Adam's family has been reunited. Evan was beyond excited, and Beth was deeply thankful for their safe return. Adam knew his family had just experienced a miracle. Their reunion was joyful, but he knew it would be short-lived as they would have to figure out their next moves in this new normal.

Carly and Carla's reunion was bittersweet. They were both truly heartbroken about the death of a wonderful man who served as their family rock. Their future was unknown. Carly was presumed dead as well as the other kids, and Carla would be declared missing when she stopped showing up for work. Hopefully, her disappearance would not cause too much of a problem for any of them.

But what about Aaron? They had put a message up to let Aaron's dad know he was safe. Obviously, Aaron wanted to get to Oklahoma to be with his own family. According to his brother's posts though, they were under constant surveillance, so their reunion would have to be postponed for a while. Oddly, his brother Danny didn't mention anything about their dad, causing Aaron's determination to get to Oklahoma soon to grow even stronger.

Juan, while mourning the loss of his parents, is determined to find his sisters. Conner and Dawn made sure he knows he has a new family now, and they would help him any way they can to find his siblings. He has a wealth of information about what the real motives of the new government are. Adam is also anxious to learn all he can from Juan and to help him any way he can with his quest to find his family.

The government has declared the kids dead, so they can't go home to Wichita. Their perceived deaths might be a blessing in disguise, or a curse if they're found. They'll have the freedom to move about through the underground railroad to help build the resistance and wreak havoc on the new governmental systems.

How strong is the new underground railroad? How big is this resistance? What can Adam do to help those out there that are trapped or lost in this new system that is taking over? Can he become the leader as he was in the previous wars he fought in? Does he want to become that man again? Have his family witness that man? War is ugly.

EPILOGUE

He never wanted his family to experience it up close and personal. Unfortunately, war seems to be already here in their new normal. How do they push this evil regime back to restore the original Constitution that this great country was founded on?

Granny has decided that the only way to survive the situation they find themselves in is to rely completely on God. While Beth and Carla tutor the kids with their regular schoolwork, Granny teaches them about God's plan for humanity.

What are the ultimate goals of this new-world order?
Are there more powerful forces at work?
Can the country survive in the *After Life as We Know It*?
Will we survive in this afterlife as they want it?
Can you survive?